His Mercy

His Guardians
Book 2

by

Ronna M. Bacon

Verses to Remember

Hebrews 4:16
Let us therefore come boldly to the throne of grace, that we may obtain mercy and find grace to help in time of need.

His Mercy

Prologue

She looked behind her as she hurried from the studio. She could hear the footsteps, but couldn't see anyone. She should have known better than to stay this late, or at least, she should have found a security guard to walk her out. Being stubborn sometimes wasn't so smart. She knew from the flowers and the boxes of chocolates with notes attached that someone wanted her dead. Now, she had placed herself in a situation where that just might happen.

He watched as she looked over her shoulder, taking care to keep in the shadows. He had her running now. Good! Soon she would run to her home town. There he would be able to find her. She had taken from him a dream he had had, and she would pay for it. He just had to decide how.

She searched the parking lot as she almost ran for her car. There were few cars in it at this time of night, and the lights weren't that bright. She had been stupid, she thought, locking her car door. She scanned the area as she started the car and hit the heater button, feeling chilled from the fright. She could feel the evil surrounding her and closing in on her. She needed to get away, to get away from this city, back to her home town. But the question she always asked, would the evil then follow her and make her run yet again, as it had for so many years and from so many places? She was tired of running.

Chapter 1

Riverville Police Chief Caleb Logan and ETF Lieutenant Doug Foster walked slowly towards the front doors of their church, deep in discussion about an upcoming concert they were expected to provide security for. The sun was hot on their heads for an early spring day and almost too bright for them as they looked around, pinpointing trouble areas. They turned as they heard footsteps behind them. Abe Finlay of Rebel's Security and his team sniper, Nathaniel Graeme, were there on the Same mission, except they had been hired to protect the pianist.

Abe studied the church and then turned to Caleb. "I never thought we'd be providing security in our church."

Caleb shook his head. "Nor did I. You two have the easy part. We have to deal with that VIP that no one wants to deal with." Caleb spoke the truth. The multi-millionaire they had to protect was in town for the concerts coming up and was insisting on having everything his way. He was a logistical nightmare for them to deal with.

"Who's the pianist?" Abe looked around as they opened the door and heard the sounds of the grand piano from the sanctuary. "We've been out of town and I just got Caleb's message this morning to meet him here."

Doug spoke up, a slightly amused tone in his

voice, knowing who the pianist was. "You'll have your hands full then, Abe. It's Whizz."

"Whizz? Really? She's back in town?"

Caleb nodded, then drew their attention to the security issues he could see.

As Abe opened the door finally to the sanctuary, they could hear their pastor, Greg Evans, teasing the pianist. They turned to focus their gaze on the front of the church for a moment, then they each turned to study the area they knew so well, but this time from a different perspective.

"Anna wants you to play the bells." Greg was teasing Elizabeth Steele, a good friend and the concert pianist who had agreed to give a free benefit concert with donations to their local food bank and woman's shelter.

"The bells?"

Greg nodded. "She wants the bells song. She is convinced that every time you play it, a whole lot of angels get their wings."

"Oh, you mean this one." Elizabeth laughed at Anna's definition of her song, and set her fingers into the hymn she loved to play, bells echoing from under her finger tips.

Greg laughed. "That's the one."

Elizabeth looked at him, a glint of mischief in her deep green eyes. "Here's one for Dad." She played out a section of Chopsticks.

Greg laughed even harder. "I'll never forget the day Mrs. C. asked you to play for everyone and that's the song you played. I thought she was going to go through the floor."

"I know. I wasn't very nice that day, was I?"

"No, but she did have a good laugh over it afterwards. You were always her star pupil."

"No, not really. Someone else was, and he wasted his talent."

Greg nodded, then as he heard the men moving around the area, said, "Drew asked for the thunder song."

"The thunder song? Your kids have such interesting titles to the hymns, don't they?"

"That they do, and I know everyone who comes wants to hear that one."

Elizabeth nodded, studied the keyboard for a minute, then set her hands to the keys. They could hear the thunder rumbling in the distance, growing louder under her finger tips, with the odd touch of rushing wind and lightning thrown in. Then, she was into the beautiful old hymn that told of the billows rising, the fear of the disciples as they cried out to the Master about the waves, and the calming of the storm. The crescendo built to a crisis, then as the chorus came, the music went soft, with only the sound of the storm coming faintly as it died away to the words whispering peace, be still.

None of the men spoke as they stopped to listen. Greg sat for a minute as she finished.

"That's the one. Drew would be pleased if you play it for him."

"Always, Greg, and I just might throw your song in as well."

"My song?"

"Yep, your song. You don't remember?"

He shook his head, wondering at what she was up to, a friend of so many years. Then he started to laugh as he heard the song. "Bringing in the Sheaves. Of course, we need that for a farmer's boy, don't we?"

He walked past the four other men with a wave and a "have fun, boys".

Caleb, Doug and Abe walked forward to greet their old friend. Nathaniel hung back a bit, awed at her talent. He studied her. She seemed so unapproachable with her classic beauty and long golden hair. He stopped near the piano. He knew he had to speak but had trouble finding his voice.

She stared at him, then pulled her reading glasses off her head and plunked them on her nose. As she turned back to her music, she asked Caleb, "Plans all in place for Sunday, Caleb?"

"As far as we can get them ready, they are."

"Good." She stared at Nathaniel again, then said, "You want my security folder, don't you?"

He nodded. "Abe needs it to finalize his plans."

She glanced past him to Abe. "He does, does he?" She spun around on the bench, hopped down the four steps and rummaged through her briefcase. Running back up the stairs to the stage, she thrust the folder at him. He grabbed it reflexively.

Seating herself back at the piano, she stated, "Caleb, I don't care where you seat that man, as long as it's out of my line of sight. The first five rows on either side are reserved for the little ones and the seniors. The next five rows are for family and friends. He counts as neither. My preference would be for you to seat him 50 miles away."

Caleb started laughing. "You know I can't do that. But I'll make sure you can't see him."

"No way to take him out before then, is there?"

Doug's "Elizabeth!" broke the silence.

She shrugged. "Just hoping. Maybe he'll break a bone and can't make it."

"Not likely to happen, Whizz." Abe studied the area again.

"Then, see that seat way up there in the back of the balcony in the corner." They followed her finger as she pointed. "I hear it has the best acoustics in the place. Seat him there."

Caleb was laughing again. "You know that won't work."

She sighed. "I know. Just hoping again. Now, if you gentleman will excuse me, I need to finalize my plans. I know you're going to want to go over plans with me too. How about lunch in an hour at Mac's?"

Abe nodded. "That we can do. Nathaniel stays here and comes with you." He reached for the folder in Nathaniel's hand, innocently avoiding the glare directed his way. "We've got confirmation you're a target again, Whizz."

She stopped moving and stared at the rugged wooden cross in front of the beautiful stained glass window behind the baptismal tank. "I know I am. I was just hoping not to have to have security here."

"Maybe when we have lunch, you'll tell us all about it. We've had bits and pieces come in over the years, but I know it's not the full story." Caleb met her eyes, not backing down. "It's time, Whizz, time for you to come clean and let us help you."

She sighed, not breaking eye contact. "I know it is. I just don't want to. He's already taken too much and I've moved too many times to count to get away from him. He always manages to find me." She turned back to the keyboard, and only Nathaniel heard her quiet whisper, "I still don't want him here."

An hour later, Nathaniel reached for her briefcase as she shut it. She stopped in surprise as he took it from her. He smiled, said nothing, just pointed to the back of the sanctuary.

She set the alarm and locked the church after them.

"Where's your car?" Nathaniel looked around, not seeing a vehicle.

"I walked."

He stopped and stared at her. "You're a target and you walked."

She glared at him. "Don't you start too. I've had enough of that. Now, give me my briefcase and I'll see you at Mac's."

He swung her briefcase away from her. "I apologize. I made an assumption I shouldn't have. Can we start over?" Gray eyes with a hint of blue met her green ones.

She narrowed her eyes, studied him and then nodded. "I guess we can." She held out her hand for him to shake. "I'm Elizabeth Steele. And you would be?"

Teeth showing white against his tan as he smiled, he shook her hand. "Nathaniel Graeme at your service, Ma'am."

She shook her finger at him. "Let's get one thing straight. I don't do "ma'ams". Got that?"

He grinned at her again. "I do. Ma'am."

She glared at him and then walked away at a fast pace. He ran to catch up, suddenly feeling a chill despite the heat of the day. He looked around. Now he knew what Matt had meant when he said he felt evil near Sarah. He could feel it, couldn't see it, but it was there.

Elizabeth walked in silence, deep in thought. She had almost forgotten about Nathaniel as he walked beside her. She shivered, knowing that she may have to face that man over the next few days and praying that she wouldn't have to. Lord, I don't want to meet him. I just can't do it. Please don't make me. I know we're supposed to forgive and move on, but I just can't. The threats from him are too real.

Nathaniel touched her elbow, and she realized he had stopped her at the cafe. She looked in through the window and then headed around the building, Nathaniel trailing after her. As she went to open a door at the back, his hand came up and stopped it.

"Why are we going in through the kitchen?" Nathaniel was truly puzzled at that.

"I will if there are a lot of people in the cafe. Mac's fine with that. I would never get to a seat if I went in the front door." She stopped and looked up at him. Goodness, she thought, he's tall. I'd get a sore neck if I had to look up at him much, and as good-looking as he is with that dark brown hair and gray/blue eyes, I would be. "Let me guess. You've never had to do security for even a low-level celebrity in the music world, have you?" As he shook his head, she continued, "Then be prepared for a crash course. People will move in on me very quickly and you're not going to be able to get between all of them and me. I usually don't have security but I am very careful to pick and choose where I go and who I go with. Right now, the cafe is full. Yes, the majority are town's people, but it won't matter. I'm the local celebrity and they feel they have the right to come up and question me and talk to me."

He waited, knowing she had more to say.

She looked up at him again, opened her mouth to speak, then shook her head. "You'll have to learn by experience. I can't explain it."

She yanked the door open and entered, leaving him to follow.

Chapter 2

Mac waved at her as she walked through the kitchen. She stopped and looked around, eyes narrowed in search, then she headed for the very back booth. Abe slid over on the seat facing the back wall, letting Elizabeth slide in next to him, and Nathaniel followed her. She was silent as she listened to the men talk, just grateful to be seated, and feeling safe for the first time in years.

Mac slid their plates of food in front of them, knowing what each one wanted without asking. He grinned at Elizabeth's silent word of thanks. He had brought her the hamburger special, knowing that she rarely ordered it outside of the cafe.

Halfway through their meal, Doug looked over at her, mischief in his eyes. "So, Whizz, have you decided on a house yet?"

She wrinkled her nose at him as she finished her mouthful of fries. "I have. The one I've been wanting for years. Joshua and Leith are both working their magic on it. It should be ready by the beginning of the month."

Caleb spoke up. "Joshua showed me the plans you came up with. Very nice. But I do have a question. Your security system? It will be a good one and up to date?"

She nodded. "I've contracted one of the best in the business. He's done work for me before. No security system is totally safe but we pray this one will be."

Caleb studied her, seeing the fatigue underlying her brightness. "Whizz, you don't have to do this alone, you know. The two men sitting with you do security for a living."

She nodded. "I know. I just.. I" She stopped, unable to continue with her words, her eyes on her plate.

Abe spoke. "It's okay. I know who you've got and he's good."

"Thanks, Abe. Now about the security at the church and the concert venue. What did you come up with?"

Nathaniel shook his head at her quick change of thoughts. He listened as they went over security, taking into account what she expected and needed.

"I guess that's it then." She sat back, picking up her cup of tea.

"Not quite." Caleb shared a look with Abe and then Nathaniel. "We're concerned for when you are out and about on your own. This person is around you when you don't see him. You need to be more than just cautious. I've taken a look at what you gave me, as had Eddie and Frankie. I've sent it on to the lab for them to look at. Why have you not told anyone?"

Elizabeth looked at him, then at Abe. "I don't think I like where this is going, Caleb."

He gave a half smile and said, "No, I don't think you will."

Abe sighed, and took up the conversation. "You need someone with you other than just for these two events. We're hoping we can corner him at one of them, but the chances are we can't. I know you're going to fight us on this one, but please listen to the plan, then decide." He held up his hand as she opened her mouth. "Whizz, please. We go back too many years for you to decide without hearing us out. At least, give us that."

She finally nodded in a disgruntled way. "Okay, seeing as you already know I won't like it, what's the plan?"

Doug smiled. "You just got yourself a new boyfriend."

Eyes round, mouth open, she stared at him and then began to shake her head. "No way, not happening."

"Elizabeth, stop. You promised you'd listen and you're not." Abe's frustration was growing. "Nathaniel will be the new man in your life. We've been hired to provide protection for you and until we catch this guy, you're our assignment."

She stared at him. "Who?"

"Who?"

"Yes. Who?"

Caleb began to laugh. "You two sound like a pair of owls. If you must know, it was Mrs. C."

"Mrs. C? She can't afford that."

"No, she can't, which is why we're doing it for her without charging her. Besides, you're our friend, Whizz. Friends protect friends."

She plunked her cup down and stared past them at the wall. "Who decided to call me Whizz ,anyway?"

Her three friends broke up in laughter at that point.

"Your dad." Abe reminded her.

"My dad?" She turned puzzled eyes to him. "I don't remember that."

"I guess he never told you, did he? He made the comment one day about how you were always whizzing here and there, just like his little sports car. That name stuck. You'll notice even he calls you that."

"I'm going to have to have a talk with him." She turned to them once more. "I need to think about this. What you're asking is hard on me, and it will be even harder on Nathaniel. I don't think you realize what it's like."

"No, we don't, and yes, you can think about it, as long as you're ready to go with the plan tomorrow." Caleb's eyes grew stern with her "We need to keep you safe, Whizz. How else can we? From what you've told me, this man finds you everywhere you go, no matter how careful you are to keep things low key and quiet."

She pointed a finger at him. "That's what I want to know. Who's telling him where I am?"

"That's something we're looking into. Eddie or Frankie are likely going to be in touch in the next day or so."

She sighed. "I knew coming back here was a bad idea. I'll never have a life again."

She shoved at Nathaniel. "Please let me up. I need to get out of here."

Nathaniel stood and then followed her as she made her way out of the cafe, again through the kitchen. She spun as she realized he was behind her.

"I haven't agreed to this yet." She was quickly losing her temper and she knew better.

"We know that, Elizabeth but whether or not you agree, I'm your bodyguard for the next few days. Please, let me do my job." He grinned at her, sun bouncing off the red highlights in his dark brown hair. "I'm not such a bad guy."

"No, I guess you're not. What is it you do any way on Abe's team?"

He hesitated, and she spun, walking away from him. "Never mind. I don't really need to know."

He ran after her, catching her arm to stop her. "It's not that I don't want to tell you, but most people don't really want to know."

"So, what is it you do?"

He sighed as he spoke. "I'm the sniper on the team."

"The sniper?" At his nod, she grinned. "Well, I've never ever had a sniper for a boyfriend. This could be interesting."

He stared at her in surprise, then when she began to laugh, he joined in.

****

He watched her as she laughed with that man. How dare she, he thought, how dare she come back here and flaunt a brand new boyfriend. I'll make short work of him. She'll pay for what she's done and so will he.

****

Doug watched them leave, amusement still twinkling in his eyes. "He's going to have his hands full."

"He will." Abe agreed. "You shouldn't tease so much, Doug."

"I know. It's like that when I'm around her. I just can't help baiting her."

"You two have always been like that." Caleb stared into the distance. "I know from her song lyrics her faith is still really strong. I have this awful feeling she's going to need her faith in a way she never has before."

Abe nodded. "I agree, Caleb. All we can do is pray for her."

Nathaniel stared at her as they neared the bed and breakfast she was staying at. "You really did mean that, didn't you?"

"About being stopped? I did. And this is mild to what I have seen. Not me, of course." She stopped and stared at the building in front of her, a frown on her face. "I just don't like being the centre of it all. I just wanted to go and write my lyrics, but then someone decided I needed to give concerts. I did that until I could get my name out there as a lyricist. Now that I have, this is the last concert set I'm giving." She looked up at him. "I just don't have it in me to give any more."

He nodded. "I know you don't. Now, what would you like to do tomorrow?"

She shook her head. "Tomorrow I just want to find somewhere quiet and relax. I'm sure all the places I used to know that were quiet aren't any more."

"I know of a spot, if you'll let me take you."

She nodded. "I can get the owner here to put up a lunch for us. And I really need to stop by the house I bought just to check in and see how things are going. Joshua promised it would be ready by the end of the month, and he has never failed to keep a promise."

Abe looked up as Nathaniel walked into his office and sat heavily in one of the easy chairs, a frown on his face. Abe sat back, waiting, knowing Nathaniel would speak when he was ready.

When he didn't, Abe spoke. "What's wrong, Nathaniel? Something's bugging you."

Nathaniel nodded, then looked up, a thoughtful look narrowing his eyes. "There is. I just can't figure out how she was found every time she moved. She was so careful, as careful as we would have been setting up security for her."

"I know. That's a puzzle. Gideon is pulling the background information on everyone in the security company."

"There has to be a leak somewhere. My gut tells me he's here in town."

Abe sighed, running his hand down his face. "I know. I think he is too. We just don't know enough about him to put a name to him yet."

"She gave Caleb everything?"

Abe nodded. "She did. She had quite a collection." He looked up at Nathaniel. "So, what's the plan for tomorrow? At least for the next few days, we're free and can watch her."

"She wants to go somewhere quiet, away from everything. After her walk home today, I agree."

Abe smiled. "I imagine that was an eye-opener for you."

Nathaniel looked at Abe, eyes wide. "It was.

Even for a little known celebrity as she calls herself, she was stopped every little while. It doesn't help she's in her hometown."

"No, it doesn't. She's one of our claims to fame, as they say. Her Dad was too, until he retired." At Nathaniel's questioning look, he continued, "Her father played back up for years in some of the big name groups. When he had health issues, about 10 years ago I think it was, he retired.

"Now about that man Caleb and his men have security for."

"That man. Who is he? She sure doesn't like him much."

Abe shook his head. "No, she doesn't. She's never said much about why, but she is adamant she has no contact with him. He's married to her Dad's sister, I think it's her third or fourth husband. A millionaire who tried to catch a ride on Elizabaeth's rising fame. She makes sure her security keeps him well away from her."

"So that's why she wanted him seated so far away." Nathaniel grinned as he remembered her comments.

Abe smiled as well. "It's up to you to make sure that he is kept away from her." He studied his friend. "Tell me, Nathaniel, are you okay with being the "boyfriend" for the next few days?"

Nathaniel shrugged. "I'm not keen on the spotlight but I'll manage." He stood. "If anything else comes up, let me know."

Abe watched as he walked away, a small smile on his face. Nathaniel seemed different tonight, a bit more relaxed. He was always intense but tonight it was tempered. Abe turned back to his paperwork, but it was a while before he picked up his pen. Time spent in prayer for his friends always helped him keep his perspective. He looked up for a minute, then nodded. Yes, Elizabeth was going to be good for Nathaniel. In fact, they would be good for each other.

Chapter 3

Nathaniel knocked at the door of the bed and breakfast and then opened the door. The owner, Lynne, went to their church and was just coming down the beautiful oak staircase in her century-old home.

"Good morning, Nathaniel. And how are you this fine day?"

"I'm good, Lynne." He looked around. "It's been a few months since you had us here for a meal. I like the updates you've done."

"I have to do them every little while to keep it fresh. Elizabeth is in the back garden. I have no idea what she's up to. Go on back through. I did leave a lunch for you two on the kitchen table."

"Thanks, Lynne. I appreciate that." Nathaniel walked through the house and out the back door, looking for Elizabeth. He didn't see her at first, then he heard her voice. Stepping away from the patio, he found her sitting cross-legged on the grass, kittens tumbling all over her. Her face was alight with laughter at their antics. He stopped to watch, soaking in how beautiful she was in the morning light, dumbfounded that she had agreed to spend the day with him, even though he was security for her.

She sensed his presence and looked up, a smile on her face. "Good morning. Aren't these adorable?"

"All of you are." He waited for her response, not

sure he should have said anything.

"They are, aren't they?" Her voice died away as she heard what he said. She looked up, her head tilted. "Flirting with me this early in the morning, Nathaniel?"

"Yes, Ma'am, I am." He grinned at her frown, then offered her his hand to rise.

She frowned at him again. "I told you, I don't do Ma'am." As she spun away from him, she continued, "I'm definitely going to have to come up with something to counteract that."

Nathaniel trailed behind her as she paced rapidly into the kitchen. Lynne stood at the counter, pastry out ready to roll for breakfast tarts for her guests tomorrow.

"Lynne, thank you for the lunch. I'm not sure if I'll be back for supper or not."

Nathaniel spoke up. "She won't be."

Lynne smiled as Elizabeth turned to glare at him. "I won't?"

Nathaniel shook his head, gray eyes sparkling with humour. "Sarah and Rebecca requested that I bring you home for dinner tonight. Abe agrees. He wants you to meet the rest of the team before tomorrow."

She frowned at him again, then smiled. "I guess I won't be home for supper, Lynne. Tell me, Nathaniel, do all the guys on your team flirt like you do?"

She spun and walked away from him, leaving him standing with his mouth open. Lynne broke out into laughter at that. Nathaniel turned to stare at her.

"That's our Whizz, Nathaniel. She's plain spoken,

does not suffer fools gladly, will staunchly defend her friends, and tease you like that if she considers you part of her family. Obviously she considers you part of her family."

Nathaniel just shook his head and followed after Elizabeth. What had Abe gotten him into?

Nathaniel closed the SUV door behind Elizabeth as they were ready to leave for Rebel's, the security compound he called home. They had spent the day wandering the woods outside of town, for Elizabeth a chance to unwind away from the people and bustle of the life she usually lived. He could see the relaxation in her face. He suddenly looked around. He could feel that chill again, the chill of evil. He couldn't see anyone, but he knew someone was there, someone who wanted nothing better than to harm Elizabeth.

****

He stood on the hill overlying the parking lot, watching, waiting. Soon, he would approach her, and when he did, she would pay for ruining his life. If anyone got in his way, they would pay too. The rage coursing through his body needed an outlet and it would come soon.

****

Elizabeth eyed the buildings of Rebel's, the compound that Abe and Rebecca's father and his brother had built to provide a secure vacation spot for VIPs. They had expanded the terms of it to provide security off site as well. Abe had taken over a number of years ago, and together he and Rebecca had decided to close down the vacation side of the business. Security kept Abe and his team of seven busy enough.

"I had forgotten how big a set up this is." She sounded in awe of it. "It's been so many years since I've been out here."

Nathaniel gave a smile. She seemed quieter than she had that morning. He mentally shook his head at her accusation that he was flirting with her. He went to deny it to himself, then stopped. Yeah, she was right. He had been flirting with her. He just couldn't believe he had. He never did that.

"They don't do the vacation side of it any more." Abe commented.

"I don't blame them. That must have been a nightmare."

"From what I understand it was. Abe wanted to tuck you away out here for the next while."

She looked at him, then back at the cottages she could see in the distance. "Not happening, Nathaniel. He would win and that I can't allow.

Rebecca, Sarah and Elizabeth had gathered at the swing at the back of the fenced yard after their supper. Rebecca had been pleased to meet the other men on Abe's team. But she needed some time with her friends. Every once in a while, the men could hear feminine laughter floating towards them.

Abe looked around him, content for now. He knew it would get intense. Elizabeth didn't know that another parcel had been delivered to her that day. Alerted by Caleb to that very possibility, Lynne had called him. The package was at the police lab even as he thought about it.

His attention turned to Nathaniel, whose eyes were locked on the women. Abe shared a look and then a smile with Gideon. In all the years he had known and worked with Nathaniel, he had never seen that look of his face. Abe turned to study Elizabeth, then studied Nathaniel. A good fit, he thought. God, thank you. Nathaniel, our intense one of the team, has found that woman You meant for him. Elizabeth will be good for him and he will be good for her.

Chapter 4

Nathaniel tapped at the door of the bed and breakfast the next morning and then entered. Not seeing anyone around, he headed for where he could hear the voices in the kitchen. Lynne and her husband were just finished clearing away the guests' breakfast.

Lynne turned and greeted him. "She's just about ready, Nathaniel. Just so you know, she's very nervous, which is not like her at all. So expect her to say anything."

"Anything?"

Adam, Lynne's husband, nodded. "When she gets nervous, she doesn't weigh her words at all. So be prepared for anything to pop out."

Nathaniel laughed, wondering how it could be any different that what he had already experienced.

He turned as he heard footsteps behind him. Elizabeth's beauty took his breath away for a minute, and then he reached for her briefcase. She gave him a shy smile, then turned to say good bye to Lynne and Adam.

"Did you bring something to change into after the concert?" Nathaniel asked. When she shook her head, he nodded at the stairs. "Go, find some clothes to take with you. We can either head for Abe's or somewhere else."

She quickly ran up the stairs and then was back in

a few minutes. He snagged the bag she was carrying and with a hand to her back, ushered her from the house to his SUV. Ian and Joseph were parked just behind him. He shut the door behind her and then stopped, staring around. He could feel the evil, almost taste it. He walked back for a quick work with Ian and then once in his vehicle headed for the church. He knew it was going to be a long day for Elizabeth and he wished he could remove the threat against her.

Nathaniel leaned against the wall in Greg's office and watched Elizabeth pace. That she was nervous was an understatement. He didn't think she was like this before her concerts. He moved away from the wall and stepped in front of her.

Elizabeth didn't see Nathaniel's move and walked right into him. His hands came to her arms to help her balance. She took a step back and looked up at him, frown in place.

"Now, that's more like it." He teased her.

"Listen, buster, I'm not nervous."

He shook his head. "Of course, you're not. You just think Greg needs a path worn into his carpet."

"Oh, is that what I'm doing?"

Head tilted, he watched as the nervousness returned. Reaching for her, he pulled her into a hug. "Let's pray, Elizabeth. Let God have your worries. The guys will do their very best to keep "that man" away from you."

She sighed, then agreed. "I know I shouldn't worry, but this time, I am. I don't know why."

"It's your home church, where you grew up. You know these people and don't want to make any mistakes in front of them. Just play your best and God will work through you."

She nodded against his chest. "I know. It sounds so simple, but it's not."

She felt herself relax as he prayed, knowing that he would continue that during her concert. She would be so glad when Tuesday night's concert was over.

A tap at the door, and Greg opened it. He studied the two of them and then shook his head.

"We're ready for you, Whizz. That is, if Nathaniel's willing to let you go."

Elizabeth blushed at his comment, then head held high, she headed for the door. Nathaniel shared a smiled with Greg, and then followed her out. He knew his teammates and those assigned from the police department were disbursed throughout the building and outside as well. He shook his head mentally at the thought that they had to go to all that trouble just for one man. Then, he felt it, felt the evil. Even in God's house, he could feel it.

Dividing his attention between Elizabeth and the audience, he could see she had them from the first note. He listened to the hymns, the scripture references, the bits of history about the hymns. Not once he noted did she mention any personal details at all. Good, he thought, someone trained her well.

Silence except for the music filled the sanctuary. Abe watched from the back as his friend played. She had a rare talent, he knew, and was sad that she was giving up her concerts. His eyes wandered the audience and then stopped and watched. He didn't know the man that his attention focused on but something seemed off. His eyes met Joseph's and

Joseph nodded. He had picked up on something as well and moved to stand near the row the man was in.

Elizabeth stood at the end of her concert, acknowledged the applause, and thanked the audience for their contributions to the projects she had targeted.

Nathaniel was waiting for her when she walked through the door towards Greg's office. His hand went out to steady her as she stumbled, spent from the emotions she had put into her music. He swept her up into his arms and then headed out the back door to his vehicle. He set her on the seat, then turned to watch the area around him. Ian handed him a bottle of juice for her and then left to wander the area.

She looked up with a word of thanks, then laid her head back and closed her eyes. He watched as she relaxed and then composed herself.

****

He watched from the sidewalk running along the parking lot. They were too close, he would never get to her. He would have to wait and waiting was not an option for him. He despised anyone who made him wait.

Chapter 5

Abe and Caleb walked towards Nathaniel, eyes searching around them. They knew he was out there, they just couldn't see him. Nathaniel moved to meet them, eyes on Elizabeth.

"How is she?" Caleb ducked his head to study his friend.

"She's exhausted and it's just not from the concert. Something is going on that she's not telling us." Nathaniel sighed. "I just wish she would open up."

Abe shook his head. "She's been like that for a long time. Part of it is being in a celebrity family. She learned early not to share a lot of private things with even her friends. I know when she was really young, someone tried to use something she said against her."

"We need to get her out of here." Caleb searched the area. "He's out there somewhere close. I can feel him."

"I know he is. I would say he's out there right now in the crowd. If we only knew who he was." Abe hesitated before he continued. "Do you think Whizz knows who he is?"

Caleb looked back at Elizabeth, then at Abe. He nodded. "I think she does. I also think she won't tell us unless she has to."

Nathaniel spoke. "I know she does." The two other men stared at him. "She made a comment the day we were checking security, something along the lines that she still didn't want him there. I can't tell you though who she was speaking about."

Abe turned as Ian came up. "We're ready to go, Abe. Just say when."

"I think now is good. We'll go out the back entrance. Caleb's had it blocked off all day. Greg's made her excuses and Lynne packed a bag for her."

Abe nodded, then took another look around. It didn't feel right having to run security at their own church, but they were taking no chances.

Later that afternoon, Abe entered the conference room in their office building and looked around. Caleb, Eddie and Frankie had joined them as well.

"I'll let you start, Caleb. You said you had news."

"I do." Caleb sat back and stared at the wall across from him for a minute, then brought his eyes back to the men seated around the table. "It's not good. I don't know how Elizabeth has kept it so quiet for so many years. She's been dealing with more than one crank."

The men shared looks with one another and then Abe spoke, "More than one?"

Caleb nodded. "That's what our lab team says. There are two that they are concerned about. No names, unfortunately, but they've given us as much information as they can. Here, this is what we've got so far."

There was silence as they read through the material. Eddie sat back, eyes narrowed, as he thought it through.

"There's one thing that puzzles me, Caleb. Why

wait until now to become so vocal and so visible?"

Frankie nodded. "That's got me puzzled as well. Why wait until she returns to her home town, unless there is something or someone here he feels may help her. Has she said anything to you, Nathaniel?"

He shook his head. "No, she's been very careful to avoid any discussion headed that way. She'll change the subject."

Caleb studied his paperwork again. "I hate to say this, guys, but this just got a whole lot bigger than what we planned for or expected. I've got pressure coming down from the mayor and town council, just to name a few people." He looked around at each of the men, stopping to study their faces. "I don't know yet what this means in terms of security for her, but I don't have the resources that are needed, and I know you, Abe, have commitments you've made."

"We do have commitments, planned training and vacations coming up over the next while. Let me work with my guys and see what we can come up with. Her Dad and Mom always welcomed us into their homes, no matter the day or time or the reason. I'd like to return the favour."

Nathaniel looked around for Elizabeth in the back yard, but didn't see her. He searched the downstairs of Abe's home and still didn't find her.

"Where's Elizabeth, Rebecca?" Rebecca was in the kitchen, going through the freezer for meat for their supper.

"She was right here ten minutes ago." She spun and ran for the stairs. "I'll check upstairs." She returned quickly. "She's not in the house and you said she's not in the yard?"

Nathaniel shook his head. "No. I don't like this."

"Nathaniel." Rebecca spoke softly and he turned. "Go easy on her. This is a really emotional time for her, even though she doesn't let it show. She hides some of her deeper emotions."

Nathaniel nodded. "If it were you and you wanted to be by yourself, where would you go?"

Rebecca smiled. Finally, she thought, a guy that gets it. "I would head for the old barn. The loft is a really great place to hide."

Nathaniel stepped out the front door, searching for Elizabeth. As he rounded the corner of the house, he saw her in the distance. Murphy and Micah were with her. He waited as the three walked towards him, the two men with impassive, grim faces. He looked at Elizabeth closely and saw what Rebecca had seen. She was also visibly annoyed at the two men with her. She brushed by him without a word. He looked after her, then back to the two men.

"Where'd you find her?"

"She was just standing near the garden area, looking totally lost." Murphy looked in the direction she had gone. "I don't know, Nathaniel. This is taking a lot more out of her than she's telling anyone."

"That's what Rebecca said. Once she gets her studio up, it will give her something to think about."

"Studio? I thought she was retiring?" Micah looked puzzled.

Murphy and Nathaniel looked at each other, realizing that a huge mistake had been made. "She's not retiring totally, Micah, just from touring as a pianist. She also writes lyrics and that's what she's planning on doing. Joshua has worked on setting up a nice studio for her."

"Maybe if you had told us, it would have helped." Micah turned and walked away in an angry manner, upset because vital information had not been shared.

Murphy looked after him and then stared at Nathaniel. "He's right, you know. Abe never did tell us that. I wonder why?" He left to find Abe and have it out with him.

Nathaniel stared after the two men, and then turned to the house, heart heavy at the discord in the team. This shouldn't have happened. Abe, what did you do?

Chapter 6

Two weeks later, Elizabeth wandered through her home, headed for her studio. She had work to do, but today she just didn't want to. She passed Micah as she walked through the hall. She knew some of Abe's men were really hesitant about her and still hadn't figured out why.

Murphy was seated in his favourite armchair in her studio, an antique one she had had re-upholstered. She had to admit, it was one of her favourite ones, too.

"Murphy, can you and I talk later? I need to find out something, and I don't want to ask Abe or Nathaniel."

He looked up at her. "Sure. Now, do you want me to sort your faxes again this morning?"

She laughed. "Sure. I know you're looking for more like you've already found."

He stared at her. "How did you know?"

"There are times you don't hide things very well, and when you find one of those faxes, your face goes all stern and dark."

He laughed. "You have gotten to know me, haven't you?"

She laughed at him as she grabbed her phone. Time for office hours and today she wanted to do nothing but hide her phone.

"Lyrics by Whizz. Elizabeth speaking." She

motioned for Murphy as she heard the voice on the other end of the phone. He walked towards her as she put the phone on speaker.

"Just where are you, Elizabeth? I need to talk to you."

"Not telling you, Grant. You're under a court order to have no contact with me."

"Yeah right. You and that other thing are going to pay for this."

Murphy's face grew grim. He listened as the conversation continued with the man's rants.

Finally, Elizabeth had had enough. She broke into his conversation and stopped it cold.

"No, you listen. This conversation is being taped. Copies will go to the police in your town and in Pat's town. Copies are also going to all of our lawyers as well as the prosecuting attorney and the judges involved. I am also giving a copy to the police where I am living now. You just blew your whole life away, buddy." She clicked off her phone, studied it and then raised her hand.

Murphy caught her hand before she pitched the phone across the room. "He's not worth it, Whizz. Let the authorities handle it." He moved her over and sat her down.

Micah appeared at the door and Murphy asked him for some water for her. He handed her a bottle, studying her as he did so. Eyes raised, he questioned Murphy with a look. Murphy shook his head.

"Stay with her, Micah. I'm calling Abe and Caleb."

Caleb looked up as Abe and Murphy entered his

office, followed by Eddie and Frankie.

"I don't like the looks of this," he commented.

"You're going to like this even less. And Whizz knows we've been pulling faxes. She read Murphy like she had known him for years." Abe shook his head. "I still haven't figured out how she does that."

"I don't think we ever will. What do you have?"

The five men's faces grew even grimmer as they listened to the taped conversation. Caleb looked through his notes and then placed a call to the police chief in Grant's town. After giving him the information and promising to send on a copy of the conversation, Caleb turned from the phone. "He's pulling him in for violating the court order. It was a pretty strict one at that."

Abe spoke up. "This really changes things. I don't think he's the one though."

"He's not." Frankie spoke up. "Whoever is sending the faxes got careless. There was a fax number at the top of one and we've been able to trace it to Oak City. The house was abandoned by the time we got there."

Eddie's face hardened. "He's likely here in town now. I've taken over the conference room again, Caleb, and have people sorting and investigating. They're not getting too far right now."

Murphy spoke for the first time. "So how do we keep her safe? We've got commitments coming up that require all eight of us to be there. And they're not short commitments either."

Abe shook his head. "We need to be there and we need to be here. And we can't clone ourselves. Let me see what I can do about bringing in someone to cover when we're away. We've got those training exercises as well."

Elizabeth was hard at work when Murphy and Abe entered her studio. She looked up briefly, waved, and then went back to her notes. She was seated at the piano, sheet music in front of her.

"Peter, there's something wrong in a couple of places. I'm not sure what you were thinking. What you have puts a sour note into it."

"Which parts?"

Murphy and Abe looked at each other. They knew that voice, a well known country star. Their respect for Elizabeth's work just rose.

"At about the two minute mark, where you take it down. Take it up a couple of notes and then down to where you started. The Same at the 4:30 mark."

"That's what I want. Thanks, Whizz. Now about the lyrics?"

"Lyrics? Who said anything about lyrics?" He laughed at her as she continued, "So what were you thinking when you wrote the tune? Any particular thoughts, verses, ideas? I have something, but I want your ideas first."

He hesitated before he spoke. "Your ideas are always spot on, I hate to suggest anything different from what you're thinking. But these are my thoughts. I've had the words surely goodness and mercy shall follow me all the days of my life. It's been way too long since I've heard one of your mercy songs. I would be honoured if you would do another for me."

Elizabeth couldn't speak and as she raised her face to stare across the room, the men saw tears on her cheeks. "Peter, this must be one of those God moments Jake's always preaching about. When I heard your tune, my thoughts went to God's mercy and how we don't deserve it. Leave it with me and I'll have something for you very soon. I already have words running around in my head."

"Thank you, Whizz. Take care."

She clicked off her phone and set it carefully on the piano. She hesitated, then jumped as a hand with a handkerchief in it appeared in her line of sight. Murphy stood her, handing it to her, a small smile on his face. She nodded thanks and then excused herself.

Abe stared after her, then turned to Murphy, shaking his head. "It's not going to be easy, keeping her safe. She knows too many people."

"That she does. So what do you suggest?"

"Yes, Abe, what do you suggest?" Elizabeth spoke from behind him. "If you're not ready to let me in on the secret, then I have work to do." She moved to brush past him, and he caught her arm bringing her to a stop.

"This stops now, Whizz. We're here because of you, because you need protection. This attitude gets lost and lost fast."

She turned to glare at him. "This is my house, Abe. I think you need to leave."

"No, we're not. There are a few people around including your parents who would like to see you stay safe and sound. Now live with it."

Murphy stared in shock at Abe's words, then his eyes turned from one to the other. Two strong-willed people battling it out he thought.

Elizabeth jerked her arm from his hand and almost ran past him out the back door. Abe sighed and then went after her. By the time he hit the back yard, she was nowhere in sight. Murphy followed on a run at Abe's yell. Where had she gone?

****

He watched as she ran from her protectors, into the woods behind her house. He followed, being careful not to make any noise. He had a good idea of where she was headed and he would be there first.

Chapter 7

“What do you mean, she ran?” Caleb was dumbfounded when Abe called him.

“We had words over whether she needed protection, which she highly objects to by the way. Before either Murphy or I could stop her, she was gone.”

Caleb stood on the back deck of Elizabeth’s house, looking around. They had not found her. Caleb was getting angry and he knew Abe was as well. Nathaniel stood beside him, not happy with Elizabeth, but he was also not happy with Abe and Caleb. He felt that both he and Elizabeth had been manipulated.

Abe stood at the bottom of the few stairs and looked up at Caleb. “She’s not here, that’s for sure.”

“I don’t blame her for running.” Nathaniel spoke, not really caring if they got mad at him. He knew other members of his team were standing around.

“Just what do you mean by that, Nathaniel?” Caleb turned on him. “She’s caused a lot of work for us.”

Nathaniel turned angry eyes on him, their heights almost matching. “Have you even stopped to think about it from her point of view? She’s come back to her home town, she’s being stalked by at least two people, no-one has been able to figure out who yet. She’s been threatened. She’s just given up a professional career that she had enjoyed, just to get out of the spotlight. She’s been drawn into a litigation that wasn't of her making." He stopped, eyes going to the house he could barely see next door. "Then you two come up with this plan for security. You never asked her, just told her how it was going to be. You decided she needed an escort everywhere when she never has in the past." He stopped again, damping down the rising anger. "She comes back to her home town and everyone treats her like she's back in high school, calling her by an old nickname she has long grown out of. You surround her with men she doesn't know and isn't sure she can trust. She has lost her trust somewhere along the line, and you two don't even see it. It's there in the little things. You think she is just being herself. She's hiding what she's really feeling, and not one person has bothered to try and find out what that is.

"You have both done her a disservice. And me, too. You never asked, Abe, if I would be willing. You just decided it would be me. Did you two even spend time in prayer over this?"

He turned and brushed past his team mates, leaving them staring after him. He was the calm, cool, and collected one on the team. They had never heard him be so vocal as he had been.

Abe stared after him, dumbfounded at the tongue lashing he and Caleb had just been given. He looked at the team members standing there, uncomfortable at hearing Nathaniel's speech. Then his gaze centred on Caleb. He nodded.

"He's right, Caleb. We did handle this differently because of who she is."

Caleb sighed, eyes on the deck floor. "Yes, he is. We can't go back and redo what we've done. We need to find her and somehow make this right and convince her to let us go ahead."

Abe snorted at that. "Yeah, good luck on finding her. She knows so many places to hide here in town, it's scary."

****

He watched from the sidewalk as Nathaniel strode rapidly and angrily down the street. He cast a glance at the house and then followed Nathaniel. Something told him a crisis had just happened, and he thought Nathaniel would be the best one to follow. He likely knew where she was. He knew she had run. He had overheard them.

****

Elizabeth sat on the park bench, tears on her face and clouding her vision. She just wanted to go back to when life was simpler, and she knew she couldn't. She was so tired right now.

God, where are You? Some days, I can't even feel You around me. I know You're there. Some days, I just want to go some place where no one knows who I am and hide. I know that's not possible. I can feel the evil closing in and I don't know who it is. I don't even know who I can trust any more. Just let me feel a piece of Your grace and mercy right now.

She sensed someone sit beside her on the bench, without saying anything. She waited, not knowing if it was friend or foe. A handkerchief appeared in her line of sight and she took it.

"Let me take you to Peg, Elizabeth." Eddie's voice was soft and full of concern.

She relaxed, knowing she was with a friend. She nodded, but made no move to rise. "How do you do it, Eddie? How do you get through the days you have with the peace I see in you?"

Eddie was silent, thinking about what she had asked, wanting to choose his words carefully. It would be nice, Lord, if You decided to help me out here.

"It's not easy, Elizabeth. Many a day, the good Lord and I have a full-day conversation. I see man's depravity in a way the average person doesn't. I have had to learn to pray about it and then leave it with Him. Having a life partner who understands and prays the Same way has been a blessing from God. He does bless us in ways we can't even imagine." He stopped and studied her profile. "You're at a point right now that you're not sure which way to run, and I mean that literally. You're getting ready to run, to leave this town. Don't. Stay and let us help you. You have someone or two to face in your life. Don't try it on your own. Come with me. I'll take you to Peg, or if you want, Ben and Marg.

"Your young man gave Abe and Caleb quite a tongue lashing, and Abe's men were there and heard it all."

Elizabeth went still. What did Nathaniel do? "What do you mean?"

Eddie smiled and patted her hand, noticing that she hadn't denied his statment. "He basically told them they were reading you wrong, that you were all grown up, and they needed to talk to you before making decisions about you and your safety. He also told Abe off for not asking if he was willing to be your daily security."

Elizabeth looked at him, eyes round, mouth open. It took a bit for her to find her voice. "He didn't, did he?" At Eddie's nod, her eyes closed. "That would go over like a lead balloon. Those two have always wanted to make the plans and have everyone fall right in with them."

"Not to worry. According to Murphy, they agreed with him. They'll be looking for you to apologize I would imagine. Now, where do you want to go? There are still guys at your house, waiting for you to return."

"I'd like to see Peg. I need one of her pep talks and hugs."

As he stood, Eddie scanned the area. He could feel someone watching, somewhere close. He waited for Elizabeth to rise and then walked with her to his car. Still looking around, he couldn't pinpoint where the danger was, but he knew it was there.

Chapter 8

Fddie knocked at Caleb's office door, and when he looked up, entered and closed the door behind him. He sank into one of the chairs in front of the desk and waited.

"You found her?" Caleb searched Eddie's face.

"I did. And you know what, Caleb, I have never ever seen Elizabeth cry. Today, I did. She was heartbroken. I don't want to ever see her like that again. She's been pushed way past her limit."

Caleb nodded, sadness in his face. "I know. We should have talked to her but there wasn't the time to go back and forth and hash out all the details that were needed. We did play the friend card, and we shouldn't have. Nathaniel made his point well."

"I would have liked to have heard him. He has come to care deeply for her. Now, he doesn't know if she would even reciprocate feelings, based on how they were brought together."

Caleb took a deep breath. "I know. Abe is trying to find him to talk with him. The other guys understand, but they're staying out of it, except for maybe Murphy. He's gotten close to her."

Eddie nodded. "Now, as to the investigation, I'm not making as much headway as I would like. We're missing something, something vital. Frankie and I are going to have to talk with Elizabeth again and see if we can clear up some questions we have." He stopped, then continued, "You do know she has that hearing next Monday she has to be at?"

"The hearing about the stolen music?" Caleb's eyes studied Eddie. There was more going on than just what Eddie was saying.

Eddie nodded. "That one. Elizabeth is really questioning her worth, her value, and where God wants her. She's past a breaking point."

"So where do we go from here? What have you gotten from the information she's provided?"

They went on to discuss the investigations. Caleb agreed that there were at least two people.

Nathaniel looked up from his Bible as Abe knocked at his cottage door. He motioned him in, not sure how Abe had taken his words.

Abe sat, staring at the floor, and rubbing his hands together.

"I need to apologize, Nathaniel. You were right. We didn't handle this well or in the proper way."

Nathaniel studied his team leader, then spoke, "Apology accepted."

Abe looked up at him. "Did you ever do something really stupid and then realized afterwards how many people you've hurt? That's how I feel right now."

Nathaniel stared down at his Bible. "I have. It's not easy asking for forgiveness. But it's what we do and what we are to extend when asked." He stopped. "Did you ever find her?"

"Eddie did. He stashed her somewhere for now and isn't even telling Caleb where."

"I bet that goes over well."

"Caleb will accept it. He knows Eddie well and knows that wherever she is, she's safe."

"Did they ever figure out anything about who it is?"

Abe shook his head. "No, I don't think they have, and that frightens me. I know she has that hearing on Monday and I'm not sure she'll even let one of us go with her."

"No, she might not and that could be disastrous. Let me talk to Eddie and get a message to her, to see if she'll talk with me."

"Please do. And if you can, tell her we're sorry and that we would like to speak with her." Abe turned and left, leaving Nathaniel staring after him. Abe seemed different and he couldn't quite figure it out.

Elizabeth turned as Nathaniel approached her. She wasn't sure she was ready to meet him again, or if he even wanted to see her.

He gave her a quiet shy smile. "Hi. I hear you ran today."

"I did. I've had enough of those two deciding my life for me." Then she stopped, horror in her face. "I didn't mean that the way it sounded. I would miss your friendship."

He breathed easily. "Thank you for that. I wasn't sure if you even wanted to see me again, given how we met."

"Sometimes God places you in situations where you have no choice or someone else is making the choices for you. It's not man's nature to like or even enjoy that. It feels like you and I are pawns in some giant chessboard, but no, I wouldn't want to not know you."

He reached for her then and hugged her. "So, then, where do we go from here?" He felt her shrug. "Will you let me go with you on Monday?"

"Monday?"

"To the courts."

"Oh that. In everything that went on today, I got word that it's been settled. His call to me was what did it. His lawyer finally got through to him."

"That's an answer to prayer. Now you don't have to be out in the public eye for that."

"I love how you think." She leaned back to look up at him. "So, I can see that brain of yours working. What are you plotting?"

"I would like to spend another day with you, doing whatever it is you like to do in your spare time."

She snorted and he laughed at her. "What spare time?" Then she looked up at him. "Okay, what I really love is just wandering through a small town, eating lunch out by a stream, and just spending time with God. Does that fit?"

"It does. Tomorrow work?"

Nathaniel stopped in the kitchen on his way out. "Thanks, Eddie."

"You're welcome. You got it all sorted out?"

"I did. By the way, let Caleb know she doesn't have the court case any more. It was settled out of court, given his call to her."

"That's good news"

****

He stood and waited and watched. Of course,

they'd stash her in an officer's house. Why would they do anything else? He turned to watch Nathaniel walk to his vehicle, searching the area around with his eyes. He knew he couldn't be seen but he still shrank back into the shadows, into the darkness. Soon, he thought, soon.

Chapter 9

Abe looked up as the men filed in for their briefing. "Where's Nathaniel?"

"He's not back?" Murphy looked around, then stepped back outside.

"What does he mean, he's not back?"

"He took off for today, just say he was spending it with a friend. He promised to be back for the meeting." Murphy had come back in. "His vehicle's not here."

Abe's heart sank. He knew then that Nathaniel had become a victim of Elizabeth's stalker. "Did he say who?"

Ian shook his head. "No, but I had the feeling it was Elizabeth. He mentioned he had seen her last night."

The men's eyes sought each other's and then turned to Abe. Abe was on the phone to Eddie.

"Nathaniel picked Elizabeth up about 9 this morning. Eddie says he has no idea where they were headed, neither one of them said."

Caleb studied the men and women gathered in the conference room, going through the pile of information Elizabeth had compiled over the years. Where were the two?

"Listen up, people. We are now taking this to the next level. Elizabeth has gone missing, as has Nathaniel. We think they're together but we're not positive on that." Caleb looked back at Abe. "Right now, we likely have a kidnapping situation on our hands. Find anything that you can."

Caleb walked back to where Abe was standing. "Have you found out anything more?"

"Not really. Micah said Nathaniel has password protection on his computer, so he couldn't access it."

"That doesn't leave us a lot of options." Caleb turned. "Eddie, how are the cell phone records coming?"

"Just got them. They're no help. Neither used their phone today." Eddie walked towards them. "I can tell you, neither said a word about where they were headed, other than they'd be back in time for Nathaniel to get to his briefing."

Caleb turned to Frankie. "Go find that aunt's husband and bring him in. Take one of Abe's guys with you."

Frankie walked into the restaurant, Murphy behind him and headed for Elizabeth's aunt. Her husband was seated facing them, and paled as they neared.

"Edward Michaels, we need you to come with us. We have some questions to ask you in an ongoing investigation."

The man stalled, knowing what they wanted. "I will come with my lawyer once I've finished my dinner. Now, excuse me."

Frankie and Murphy stood, patiently waiting. The man made no effort to rise. Finally, Murphy walked over to him, bent to speak quietly in his ear, and straightened back up. Michaels paled even more, then excused himself to his wife. "I don't know when I'll be home. I'm sorry, my dear."

His wife watched as he disappeared out of the restaurant. Frankie shut the back door of the cruiser behind him, then turned to Murphy.

"What did you say to him to get him to come?"

Murphy looked away, a sadness crossing his face. He then looked back at Frankie. He drew a deep breath before speaking. "I just asked him how old she was when he made his pass at her and if he wanted me to tell his wife there in the restaurant."

Frankie sank back against the cruiser and stared at Murphy. "How did you know?"

Murphy shrugged. "There's not much that would send Elizabeth running from him like she has, or develop such a great dislike for him. I took a guess."

"And guessed right." Frankie stepped away from the cruiser to stare through the window. "No wonder she hates him."

****

He had searched everywhere for her. Where was she? She wasn't at home. She wasn't at Rebel's Compound. She wasn't at Eddie's. So where was she? He needed to find her and soon.

****

Nathaniel stood from the chair he had been shoved into and walked around the room. There was not a lot of furniture, and what there was had a rough feel to it. He looked for anything he could use for a weapon and found nothing. He tried the windows. He couldn't open them, but he would break one of them if he could. It wasn't that big a drop to the ground. He just needed to find Elizabeth. He knew she was around here somewhere. It had scared him when he looked up yesterday and saw her with the man's arm around her and a knife to her throat. He had had no choice but to go along with him. He had felt the weapon at his own back.

He sat back down and tried to figure out a way to escape. It wouldn't be easy. It had been dark in the building when they brought them through, locking him in one room and Elizabeth in another. He prayed she was safe.

God, where are you? his heart cried. Why have you allowed this to happen? Keep Elizabeth safe.

Elizabeth roused. She had fallen asleep even though she hadn't wanted to. She raised herself and looked around. Just what she thought. Some abandoned or next to abandoned building. She had recognized the voice of the man behind her. Her aunt's husband was behind this, she knew. That man worked for him.

She paced the floor, trying to find a way out. She didn't want to face him, didn't want to see him at all. She had been running from him for too many years now.

Where was Nathaniel? She prayed he was alive, that they had not hurt him. She turned as she heard the lock turn at the door, and the door opened, heart in mouth that it would be him.

The man from the day before stood in front of her. Not speaking, he jerked his head that she was to come. She stood rooted to the floor, afraid to follow him. He strode angrily across the room, and jerking her arm, forced her out the door. She heard a door behind her and then Nathaniel's foot steps. He was still alive. Thank you, God.

They were forced down the stairs and back into the

vehicle. Not a word was spoken as they were driven away from the house and towards the forest. Nathaniel reached for her hand and held it in his strong grip. No matter what happened, he would do his best to protect her.

The vehicle stopped and they were forced from it. Hand in hand, they were made to walk into the forest. Elizabeth drew closer to Nathaniel. She didn't like the feeling she was getting. Lord, protect us. Keep us safe.

Abe turned to his men gathered, ready to board their jet. "I know we're missing Nathaniel. He's in our prayers. Let's get in and get out as quickly as we can. If things go as planned, we'll be home this time tomorrow. Let God go before us."

The men were quiet as they boarded, Ian and Murphy heading for the cockpit. Ian settled behind the wheel and after going through his preflight routine, he turned to Murphy. "I don't like leaving Nathaniel here."

Murphy nodded. "Me, neither, but this time we have no choice."

Caleb looked up as Frankie entered his office. It was late and he should already have left, but he waited to hear what Michaels had said.

"Did you get anything?"

Frankie shook his head. "He asked for a lawyer right away and the lawyer has refused to let us talk with him. We'll have to let him go soon, unless we can find something definitive to charge him with."

Eddie knocked at the door and spoke. "We just did, Frankie. Evidence he was involved in murder and kidnapping a few years ago. I have a feeling this is how he's made his money."

Caleb stood. "Let's get what we need from the judge and then go bring him to an interrogation room. I just hope he's willing to cooperate, but somehow I don't think he will."

Chapter 9

Nathaniel moved, pain wracking his body as he rolled to his side. He wasn't sure where he was and as he tried to lift his head, blackness swirled, threatening to engulf him again. He fought back against it and won. Sitting up took effort and his hand went to his ribs. Bruised, cracked, maybe fractured. He couldn't tell for sure, but he knew it was one of those choices. Squinting he looked around. Where was he? Then he stilled. Where was Elizabeth? He spun around to look, and once again blackness threatened to engulf him.

She wasn't with him. Where was she? They had been together when he had been shoved over the side of the cliff. Thankfully it wasn't a long fall, but it had been enough to knock him out. He staggered to his feet. He needed to find her. Darkness was coming, and he could feel the dampness of the coming rain. Which way, Lord, which way do I go?

He stood and waited, then moved forward, confident he had been given the right direction to go. As he searched along the bottom of the cliff, he saw her. She was crumpled near some trees, not moving.

He dropped to his knees and with a shaking hand, felt for a pulse. His head dropped and he breathed a prayer of thanks. She was alive. He quickly assessed for broken bones but didn't think she had any. He sat beside her and pulled off his jacket, covering her with it. He shivered in the wind and looked around. He didn't dare move her, but how long would it take for help to come when no one knew where they were?

He stumbled to his feet again and gathered wood together. He still had his matches at least. They hadn't taken them from him.

Eddie and Frankie stood outside the house and watched the activity.

"They were here." Eddie turned to scan the area. "Somehow, he got word out to move them. But where to?"

"We need to bring his lawyer in. That's the only way he could have gotten word out."

Eddie nodded. "Now that's a man I would like to see go down. He's been riding right at the line for years. This time, he stepped over it."

"That he has." Frankie stepped away as one of the officers came up to him.

"Eddie, I think we've got something. A neighbour saw a vehicle pulling out of here this morning and heading towards the woods over on 20."

Eddie stared at Frankie. "That's a big woods, with lots of cliffs."

Frankie nodded. "I know. We'll need the search and rescue crew for sure. If you can make that call, I'll call Caleb with an update."

They stood in the dusk at the staging area, handlers and dogs moving around the parking lot, waiting for word to move out. Caleb stared around, not sure if they were in the right spot, but with nothing else to go on they had to start somewhere. He turned as an officer ran towards him.

"They've picked up their scent, heading into the

woods.”

Activity picked up and the search teams headed out, each accompanied by an officer. Caleb heard for the command centre, knowing that’s where he needed to be. He stopped as he saw Eddie approaching him.

“What’s up, Eddie?”

“We just got word the lawyer was killed earlier today.”

Caleb’s eyes slid closed, and then he nodded. “Any way to connect it with Michaels?”

“Not yet, but that’s the assumption we’re working on.”

Nathaniel looked up through pain-filled eyes as a shape emerged from the darkness. The man’s hands reached for him and steadied him as Nathaniel stood.

“Steady, lean on the cliff, son. Let me check your friend. Then we’ll move to better quarters.”

Nathaniel watched as the man knelt by Elizabeth and assessed her condition. When he stood, he stared around, then moved to put out the fire Nathaniel had built.

“I’ll take you to my cabin. It’s not far. With the rain moving in, you two would never survive out here. I saw your fire and knew no one was out here earlier.” The man swept Elizabeth up into his arms, then turned to Nathaniel. “Can you walk?”

Nathaniel hesitated then nodded.

“Grab hold of my coat. I’ll walk slow. I don’t want to lose you in the darkness. There are too many places you could fall into. You were wise to stay where you were.”

Nathaniel stood wavering in the cabin, watching as

Elizabeth was laid on the only bunk. The man turned to Nathaniel, then reaching for a blanket, wrapped it around him and shoved him into the only easy chair, near the fireplace.

The man moved away and then came back with a towel and a mug of something hot.

"Here, drink this. It will help to warm your insides."

Nathaniel took it and sniffed it, then sipped. Broth the likes of which he had never tasted before. He drank, setting the mug down when it was half empty. He used the towel on his hair and face, laying his head back when he was finished. He was suddenly exhausted, unable to keep his eyes open any longer. He slept, not seeing the man come back to check on him and remove the mug and towel. The man studied him and then nodded. Nathaniel would sleep the night away, with what he had slipped into the soup.

The man turned his attention to Elizabeth. He sat on the edge of the bed and studied her face. He knew who she was, had seen her around town, had attended many of her concerts. He knew her father well. She was safe for the night, he thought. Tomorrow would come and then he would see about getting them out. He pulled the blankets up on her and then reached for his medical supplies to tend the wound on her head.

Caleb turned as the dogs and their handlers made their way back through the pouring rain. They had lost the scent. They would be back in the morning, hoping the rain had let up and see what they could pick up.

"Are there any hunt camps or cabins people might still be using this late in the season or early for some?"

Eddie nodded. "There are a few scattered around. In fact, I know of one not far from here but it's not safe to try and get to at night, not unless you know the area real well and I don't think any of us do. I can head out there in the morning." He turned to study Caleb. "Make sure you get some sleep tonight, Caleb. And make sure you make your peace with God. Elizabeth would want you to do that." He walked away, Caleb staring after him.

How does he do that, Caleb wondered, hit right where you're hurting. He's so spot on, God. I do need to make my peace with you over what I did with Elizabeth. Then, I need to make my peace with her. Keep those two safe this night.

He turned and walked back to the command centre. It was going to be a long night and he would try to catch some sleep as he could.

Abe turned as Murphy sat in the seat beside him. He waited, knowing Murphy was mulling something over in his mind.

"Do you think they've found them yet?"

Abe shook his head. "I haven't heard but I pray they did. We had some nasty weather moving in overnight and I hope they aren't out in it.

****

Where was she? Was she out in that storm? If she died, good riddance, but it wouldn't solve his problem. He needed her alive.

Chapter 10

Abe stood waiting for Caleb to come towards him. He knew the rest of his team would be there as soon as they had settled away the equipment they had used in their mission. Usually he was the one leading this, but Murphy had taken over and sent him and Micah on ahead.

Caleb approached Abe, not quite sure how to talk to him. Abe reached to shake his hand, and then studied the woods.

"Any idea at all where they might be?"

Caleb shook his head. "The rain last night pretty much wiped out any scent trails there were. The dogs have been out again but the handlers aren't optimistic. Eddie knew of a cabin nearby and was headed out there with Micah. Other than that, it's going to be leg work and a lot of that."

"My guys are heading this way once everything is squared away. They'll help wherever you need them."

"Thanks. Abe." Caleb hesitated to speak and Abe looked over at him. "I'm sorry I got you involved the way I did. I just didn't follow protocol quite the way we normally do. Yes, we have stepped in like this before, but I should have taken the time to talk to Elizabeth."

"You and me both, Caleb. We share the blame. Let's just we've apologized and it's in the past for us.

Now to find those two." Abe walked away to meet his team, Caleb staring after him, wondering how he had gotten to that point so quickly while he still struggled.

Nathaniel stirred, feeling warm and more alert than he had the night before. His eyes slid opened and he stared at a fireplace he didn't remember seeing last night. He sat upright, waiting for the spinning in his head to stop and stared around. He was in a cabin. How had he gotten here? The last he remembered was building a fire beside Elizabeth. Elizabeth! Where was she? He stood, entangled in the blanket he had been wrapped in, and searched the cabin. There she was, on the bunk.

He shook off the blanket and stumbled to her side, sinking to the floor. He reached out a trembling hand and felt her face. It was cool but she had a large bandage on the one side. He couldn't remember what had happened. He remembered them spending the day wandering through the small town, eating near the river, and then nothing. He had no idea what day it was either.

He watched her sleep. It was sleep, he could tell, and not that she was unconscious. What was going on? He turned as he heard steps behind him.

The man from the night before stood near him, silent and watching. He held out a mug for Nathaniel, who hesitated.

"Go ahead, take it. It won't put you to sleep this morning. Your friend has already had something to drink and gone back to sleep." He reached out a hand to help Nathaniel stand. "Careful, you're not quite steady on your feet yet."

Nathaniel sank back into the chair. "Who are you?"

The man sat on a stool in front of the fireplace, which burned at a low level. He took a sip from his own mug, all the while studying Nathaniel. He finally nodded and set his mug down on the stone hearth.

"My name is Jake. I've been a friend of Elizabeth's family for years, although not many people would know that. Every year, for about two months, I escape to this cabin. God had me come late this year, and it was because of you." He peered intently at Nathaniel. "Maybe you can tell me why."

Nathaniel went to shake his head, then regretted it. "I can't remember how we got out here. It's just a big blank."

Jake nodded. "That's what I figured. You've got quite the knot on the back of your head. How be you tell me who you are and how you're connected to Elizabeth?"

Nathaniel drew a deep breath, decided he could trust Jake, and told him the story of what was going on. Every once in a while, Jake would nod or ask a question. When he was finished, Jake stood and walked over to check of Elizabeth. He returned and once again sat on the stool.

"Have they arrested Michaels yet?" At Nathaniel's puzzled glance, he continued, "Elizabeth's aunt's husband. He's been involved in kidnappings and murders for years but in such a way there was never any proof. I figured that's how he got his money. I know Elizabeth doesn't like him, and if what I have seen of him making passes at young women is what he did to her, then it's a good thing he's not sitting here."

Nathaniel's eyes slid closed. "Do you really think that's what was going on?"

"Knowing him, I would hazard a guess that it was. She's real uncomfortable around him and has avoided being at as many family get-togethers as she could if she knew he would be there. I would say she never said anything to her parents." Jake picked up his mug. "Now, we need to figure out how to get you two out safely. Not knowing who pushed you over the cliff makes it difficult."

Nathaniel swallowed hard. "Pushed over the cliff?"

Jake nodded. "It's that or you two just walked off the edge, and somehow I don't think you did that." He looked over as Elizabeth stirred, then rose and went to her.

Elizabeth blinked as she roused back to consciousness. Where was she? She stared around, trying to bring everything into focus, then shrank back as she saw a man approaching her.

He knelt by her bed and spoke. When she didn't respond, he spoke again.

"Elizabeth."

She turned, not quite hearing what he said.

"Elizabeth."

This time, it was clearer and she knew the voice.

"Jake?"

"Yeah, it is, honey. You're in my cabin, and your sweetheart's sitting over in my chair."

She frowned at him. "Sweetheart. Who's that?"

Jake shook his head. "You don't remember?"

She closed her eyes as she waited for her head to clear more. "Yes, I do. Nathaniel. Is he okay?"

"He's fine aside from a bump on the head and some sore ribs. About the same as you. Can you tell me how you got out here?"

She frowned, then spoke. "I could use a cup of your coffee, Jake. No one makes it like you do. And I could also use some help to sit up."

Nathaniel stood behind Jake. "I'll help you up as Jake makes his coffee for you."

Jake moved away, pretending not to notice the looks between the two. Nathaniel reached and helped Elizabeth sit up and kept an arm around her as she waited for her head to stop spinning. She rested her forehead on his shoulder and sighed.

"Did we really get shoved off that cliff?" She felt his shrug. "You're not going to tell me you don't remember."

He helped her to stand and wrapped a blanket around her, sweeping her into his arms and then depositing her in his chair. "I could, but I won't, seeing as you've already figured that one out."

"Great, now I have to live with that memory for both of us."

Jake handed them each a mug. "What do you remember?"

"Not a whole lot. I can remember a car ride from a house, walking for a while, and then being pushed off the cliff. They pushed Nathaniel first." She looked up, tears in her eyes. "I know who the men are and who they work for."

"Michaels." It was a statement from Jake, not a question.

"It was. I've always been afraid he would try something like this. He doesn't like taking no for an answer and I refused him years ago."

"This time, he's stepped over the line. Caleb will make sure he never hurts anyone ever again."

"I've heard rumours for years about his activities. How can Aunt Amy stay with him?"

"He has likely spun a tale to explain it all away. I have seen her look at him sometimes, and it makes me wonder how much she suspects or knows."

Chapter 11

Jake turned as he heard footsteps approaching the cabin. "You two stay here. Not a sound."

He grabbed his rifle, settled his hat on his head, and stepped outside, carefully closing the door behind him. He settled down on a stump near the edge of the clearing, a favourite spot for him to sit and think. He watched and waited as the careful footsteps approached.

"Well, Eddie, it's been a long time since you've been out here."

Eddie stopped, searched the area, then came towards him, Micah following. He reached to shake Jake's hand and then introduced Micah to him.

"You're here late this year, Jake." Eddie scanned the area out of habit.

"I am. The weather had us cancelling some concerts and we made them up at the end of the trip. We're not planning a concert tour this year, just studio work, and it doesn't start until the fall. It has worked out well for me to be here now." Jake gave a half-smile. "They're here, Eddie, battered and bruised but alive."

Eddie nodded. "I was praying you found them. The Lord must have wanted you here this year at this time."

Jake looked up at the brightening sky, then around the clearing. It was early spring, the flowers just starting to poke their heads through the moulding leaves, as were the new saplings. He could hear the birds chattering and singing away as they worked on their nests, could hear the whispers of sounds from the other creatures that co-inhabited the space with him.

Micah studied the man in front of him. There was no way he could believe this was a well-known singer, just sitting there chatting with Eddie as if he had no care in the world.

Jake laughed. "Sorry, Micah, I'm really him. This is me being myself."

Micah shook his head. "I don't know how you guys do it."

"Do what?" Jake asked, an amused tone in his voice.

"Read minds."

"It comes with age and practice and sometimes a little help from God."

Nathaniel studied the woman sitting in front of him. She turned as she felt his eyes on her and tilting her head, studied him back.

"So, where do we go from here?" Nathaniel was hesitant to ask.

She shrugged. "I don't know, Nathaniel. They've caught one of them but there's another one out there. I'm done with Caleb and Abe and their security. I should never have agreed to it in the first place."

"No, you should have been given a choice, and I told them that."

She choked on her coffee. "You did what?" She had forgotten that they had talked about this.

"I told them they should have talked to you and given you a choice. That they did a disservice to us both. They didn't give us a choice as to whether you wanted an escort, or who it should have been."

She studied him once again, looking deep into his heart and soul, and pondering his words. She gave a small smile. "I would have chosen you."

He stopped and looked at her, then smiled. "Thank you. When this is all over and done with, I would like to spend time just getting to know you and you getting to know me." He reached over and dropped a kiss on her cheek.

She reached and placed her hand on the spot, astonishment in her eyes. Any other man would have aimed for the mouth and she would have no part of that.

Nathaniel smiled once again. "You're surprised. Don't be. Your kisses are yours to give and it is your decision who you give them to."

"Thank you, Nathaniel. You're so different from the men I've met in the past twelve years."

They both turned as the door opened and the three men walked in. Eddie assessed them, then nodded. Jake had been right in his assessment.

"Ready to go home?" Eddie walked through to the kitchen, grabbed a chair and came back to sit with them.

Micah leaned against the wall, watching, on guard. He too could feel the evil and wanted to make sure nothing happened again.

"Not on the terms I was under, Eddie. I'm done with that." Elizabeth refused to back down.

"I understand. We'll work something out, but this time you have final say." She stared at him, not quite sure if he was telling her the way it would be. "We're serious this time, Elizabeth. Caleb and Abe both know they made a mistake with you. Caleb did act with proper police authority, but maybe not in the wisest way when it involved a long-time friend.

"And you, Nathaniel. You weren't treated fairly. You weren't given a choice and they know that."

Nathaniel held up his hand. "It's okay, Eddie, really. We've talked and worked things out, the two of us."

Eddie smiled. "I knew you would. Just wanted you to know how I felt."

"Well, it was kind of obvious when you hid Eizabeth and refused to tell them where she was." A hint of a grin peeked through the grimness on Nathaniel's face. He looked over at Micah, then stood, wavering for a minute until he got his balance. Motioning to the door, he left the cabin, Micah behind him. They had a discussion to have and he would just as soon not have anyone overhearing it.

Eddie watched as the two men left. "He's hurting."

Jake turned and looked at the door. "He is. He doesn't remember anything about the abduction or what happened until he roused at the bottom of the cliff. He may never."

****

He stood in the parking lot, staring around. They were gone, the police, the search and rescue, the dogs, the command centre. Did that mean they had given up or that they had found them? He threw the rock he was holding across the parking lot, hearing it bounce off a tree. He was beyond frustrated. She wasn't anywhere he could find her.

Chapter 12

lizabeth sat in her studio, surrounded by sheets of music. She needed to work, but her mind wasn't on lyrics. She stared at the picture across from her, not taking in any of the details. She looked back down, sighed, gathered up the music and walked to the piano. Spreading it out on the book rack, she studied it. Lord, I need some inspiration and I am not sure where to go for it. These past few days sort of broke my train of thought. Your mercy - that's what I need to write about but how can I when I need to show mercy to my friends? Lead in that, Lord, help me to forgive.

She bent her head once more and let the verses she had been studying on mercy flow through her mind. She reached for the music sheets and studying them, playing out the notes in the treble cleft. She could hear movement outside of the closed doors to her studio and tried her best to ignore it.

Finally, she was able to set the outside world aside and concentrate. As always, the words flowed from her pen and as she set them to music, the rich tones of the song flowed through her home.

Abe stood and listened as Elizabeth sang the words, went back and forth with what she was writing. Mercy, he thought, God's mercy is given so freely, but we take it for granted. Lord, forgive me. That's what I did with both Elizabeth and Nathaniel. We need to heal our friendship.

Nathaniel stood, the latest threats in his hand, anger building inside him. Who was this person and what was he really after? He looked up to see Abe approaching and thrust the papers at him.

"Have you seen these?" His voice taut with anger, he could barely speak.

Abe shook his head. "More threats, I take it."

Nathaniel nodded. "We need to catch this guy, but how do we do it?"

Abe took the pages from Nathaniel, and frowned as he read them. He turned to look at the studio door. "I hate to disturb Elizabeth, but I think it's time we sat down with her and went over everything. We're missing something and I just don't know what it is. Caleb, Eddie and Frankie feel the same." He stopped. "I hate to have her go over all this."

"Don't sell her short, Abe." Nathaniel studied his team leader and friend. "She'll run again and this time we won't be able to stop her or help her in time."

"That's what I'm afraid of. If she runs, he'll get her and we'll never find her." Abe turned to Nathaniel. "How's the head?"

"It's getting there. You're worried about the assignment coming up in a couple of days, aren't you?"

Abe nodded. "I need you with us, but I won't let you go if you're not 100%. Have the doctor give you another examination tomorrow. We'll decide from there." He sighed as he turned to the studio door. "I hate this part. She should be able to create without this guy disturbing her."

Elizabeth didn't hear the knock at the door or Abe opening the door and the two men entering. She stared at them, then looked away, lost in the lyrics she was composing. Then she looked back and frowned.

"What are you two doing here? I don't like the look of that face, Abe?"

"Can you spare some time, or do you need to finish what you're working on?" Abe hesitated, not knowing how she would react to him any more.

"Actually, they're done. I just need to polish a bit but they're about where they should be." She looked up at them again. "So, what do you have there?" She reached for the papers.

"I hate to show you these, Elizabeth, but we need your help. We've tracked down as much as we can, even with the IT working on it. We're at a standstill."

"And you're hoping I can remember something that will start up the process again?" She smiled. "Relax, Abe. Anger is over, let's move on. Now, I do have a file of those who didn't send in threats or warnings but we felt they needed closer watching." She jumped from the bench, crossed to the filing cabinet, and pulled open a drawer.

Nathaniel reached for the file. "It's thick."

"Yes, it is." Elizabeth shook her head. "Being a celebrity, even a low key one, is no fun."

Caleb looked up from his neverending paperwork as Frankie knocked at his door. "What's up, Frankie?"

"Abe's brought Elizabeth in to go over the massive amount of paperwork that's accumulated. He's got more threats today. She's brought in a file that she's kept over the years of possibilities. I've passed it on to the team."

"Where is she?" Caleb rose, stretched and then headed for the door.

"She's in the conference room. She refused to be anywhere else."

Caleb nodded. "No, she shouldn't be there, but it's her life and we need to get it back for her. Abe's away again in two days, isn't he?"

"That he is. Where are we going to put Elizabeth to keep her safe?"

"That's the million dollar question. I don't think she'll leave her home again."

Nathaniel watched as Elizabeth worked her way through the stack of notes she had been handed. He didn't like the look on her face, the pale and drawn look of someone hurting.

She looked up, staring into the distance, then handed him the sheets of paper. She stood and walked away, out of the room. He dropped the paper and followed her. She paced the break room, avoiding the officers who were moving around. Then she turned to him.

"Nathaniel, I need to go somewhere and it will take a couple of hours to get there. Can you clear it with Abe to go with me?"

He nodded, then turned to find Abe standing beside him.

"Go with her. Take Micah as well. He's outside waiting."

Nathaniel reached for Elizabeth's hand and pulled her through the department and out the door. Micah held up his keys and they headed for his vehicle.

"Where are we headed, Elizabeth?" Micah turned

to watch her as she seated herself in the back seat.

"Oak City for starters. I'll give you the directions as we get closer. I'm not sure of the street address, but I know how to get there."

****

He stood and watched them leave, then headed for his own car. He would follow and see where they were going. He needed to stop her, stop the investigation, and get what he wanted and needed from her. But how could he get close to her?

Chapter 13

"It's there on the right, Micah." She reached for the door handle and was out of the vehicle and into the building before either man could stop her.

Micah reached and caught Nathaniel's arm before he could open the door. "I think she wants us to wait here."

Nathaniel leaned back against the seat, eyes constantly moving to watch the area. "I know. I just wish she had let one of us go with her."

"She can probably move faster on her own, and she needs to in this area of town." Micah looked around. It was not one of the better areas of town.

The back door opening caught their attention and they both turned to see Elizabeth sliding back into the vehicle. "I got it. Now, we have to go to the bank on Montgomery. There's more stuff there in the box."

Nathaniel stared at her. "How much do you have?"

"Too much," Elizabeth said sadly. "Way too much. Stop here, Micah. I'll be about 10 minutes."

Nathaniel stopped her from opening the door. "This time, I'm going with you. I won't take no for an answer."

She glowered at him, then abruptly nodded. "I've been looking after myself for years, you know. I don't need a babysitter."

Micah tried hard to hide his grin. Nathaniel glared at him as he opened his door.

Micah watched as they crossed the parking lot to the bank, then stepping from the vehicle, kept an eye on the area. He could feel something, he wasn't quite sure what. There was nothing overt that he could see, but he knew someone was there. He turned as he heard footsteps approaching. Elizabeth had been right, she hadn't needed a long time in the bank.

"Where to now, Elizabeth?" Micah asked as he pulled away from the bank.

"Coffee, please."

The men shared a glance and then shrugged. If she wanted coffee, so did they.

"And make it a drive-through, please. I don't want to get out."

Elizabeth's hands rested on the material she had gathered. She wasn't ready in her mind to open the box that would be opened, but in her heart, she knew she had to. She was sure others had been the victim of this man. She had to stop him.

Nathaniel looked in the side view mirror. "I would say we have a tail."

Micah nodded, eyes searching for a way to get rid of it. "I do, too. Elizabeth, how well do you know this area?"

She shrugged. "Well enough I guess. Why?"

"We have a shadow and I want to ditch him."

She turned to look out the back window, then looked ahead. "There's a street coming up on the right. Take it. Then a sharp left, then another right, then a right. That will bring you back to here. When you get back to this road, go straight through the intersection to the second left. Take it. It will lead to the major road to the highway. Not a lot of people know that."

"I think that worked, Elizabeth." Nathaniel was searching behind him. "I don't see him."

"No, but he'll likely be waiting for me at my house." Elizabeth kept the shudder she felt from showing.

"We're heading for the police department with that material. Then we'll figure out what to do with you." Micah turned a grim look to Nathaniel, who nodded.

"Not happening, Micah. I'm through hiding."

The two men shared a look, and then Nathaniel glanced back at Elizabeth. He needed to keep her safe, but it would be so difficult now that she had decided she wasn't running any more.

Elizabeth shoved the new material at Eddie. "Here, add this to your pile. It's not only on me this time. There are others involved who had been threatened. There's about six of us who had had the same or similar threats. We hired someone a few years ago but he got nowhere. It was almost as if he thought we were making it all up and sending ourselves the letters, just to increase our popularity. I never felt comfortable that he had done a thorough job." She turned and almost ran from the room.

Nathaniel headed after her, catching up with her just outside the department front door. He reached for her hand and pulled her down the street.

"Where are we going, Nathaniel?"

"I have it on good authority that chocolate makes all things better. So tell me, does it?" He grinned at her look of exasperation.

"I have no idea. I don't do chocolate."

"There's quite a list of things you don't do. How about ice cream? Do you do ice cream?"

"If I say no, what's your next suggestion?"

"How about an English tea?"

She looked at him. "Really? There's a tea room here?"

He nodded and led her down the next street, stopping in front of a non-descriptive shop. He opened the door and ushered her inside. "Here. I discovered this by accident one day. The tea is here really good."

Nathaniel headed for a table at the back of the tearoom. After seating her at a table for two, he slid into the chair across from her.

"May always has a great selection of goodies to go with a wide selection of tea. I stop in here every once in a while." He watched her face, seeing the fatigue in it.

"Thank you, Nathaniel. This is nice." Elizabeth looked around at the room, taking in the decoration. Then her eyes centred on the piano. "They have a piano here."

Nathaniel laughed. "And if you ask real nice, May might let you play it."

"That I would, Nathaniel. Elizabeth is always welcome to it." Elizabeth looked up, recognizing the soft voice with the British accent as a friend of her mother's.

"Thank you, May. This is really nice."

****

He sat at a table near the front of the tearoom, seated so he could watch her. He resented that she was there with him. He needed to get to her and couldn't when she was surrounded by so many. Then, a thought crossed his mind. He would have to think through what he wanted to do, but it just might work.

Chapter 14

Caleb looked at the tables that had the documentation spread out on it. He knew there was even more at the lab.

"Where do we stand, Eddie?"

Eddie turned from a table that held photos. "We're finished sorting by document type and by person. That has then been sorted by date as much as we can." He shook his head. "There is just so much, and so many people. Too many. We'll need to work on narrowing that down, and that is going to take time. We're also looking at cities where the material was mailed from, if we know that, and where it was received."

"Who can we free up to start data entry on this and run it through some of our programs? We should be able to sort through it a lot faster that way."

"Good thought. I'll see who we have that can do that. We're looking at probably 10 years' worth of paperwork, likely 5 or 6 that are high on the list for possible suspects, and even those lower on the list can't be excluded." He stopped and turned to Caleb. "And there is no guarantee he is even in this pile of paper."

"Now, that I don't like to hear." Caleb turned as an officer approached, holding out a file. "What's this?"

"I think you need to see this. This was buried

down in the paperwork from about five years ago. It's very scary."

Caleb studied the grim face of the officer, then took the folder. He opened it and began to read. He stopped, looked for a chair, and sat. Eddie watched his face grow even grimmer. When Caleb looked up, there was anger in his eyes.

"This is just sick, Eddie, just plain sick." He handed the file off to him and rising, walked away.

Eddie watched him go, then opened the file. I agree, Caleb, this is just plain sick. To threaten someone in this way is just unthinkable. He turned to search the room, then approached one of the female lab techs.

"Carrie, this is brutal, but can you take it and see what you can find from it? The envelope is there as well as the letter."

"Sure, Eddie. Give me a couple of hours and I'll have a preliminary report for you, I hope." She turned back to the computer she had been using.

Eddie turned, suddenly feeling the need to get out of the room and spend time with his God. Lord, this is just so awful. How depraved is man now. Protect my friend, Elizabeth, and those who provide her protection. Guide us as we search for this monster, as monster he is.

****

He followed them out of the tearoom and down the street. Where were they heading? He didn't see one of their vehicles, so they were walking. He turned and headed back. Now was not the right time. He would have to wait and he hated waiting.

****

"What time do you leave in the morning?" Elizabeth stood by her car, looking up at Nathaniel.

"Really early, like about 3 tomorrow morning. We'll be gone for about a week or so, Abe thinks." He stared off in the distance, then looked down at her. "Please stay safe, Elizabeth."

She nodded. "You, too. Maybe by the time you come back, this will be all over."

"It would be nice, but I doubt it will be. There's a lot of material to go through."

He watched her drive away, then turned to his own vehicle. He really didn't want to leave her right now, but he had no choice. He needed to get his head back to where he needed to be.

A week later, Abe stood and watched as his team sorted through their equipment and stored it away. He could see the fatigue in their movements. Somehow, he had to stop this long flights. They were wearing out under them. This time, it seemed as if anything that could go wrong, had gone wrong. He turned to head for his office.

Abe looked up at a knock at his office door. Murphy stood there and entered when Abe beckoned. He sank heavily into one of the chairs and then stared at the floor

"What's up, Murphy?"

Murphy looked at Abe. "I feel like we were set up on this one, Abe. It should have been a smooth assignment and it wasn't. The men are hurting badly over this one."

Abe sat back. "That's how I feel. But who would do that to us?"

Murphy shrugged. "That's what I can't figure out, who?"

Abe nodded. "We need to have a team meeting in the next few days. Let's take some down time over the next few days and regroup Monday morning. They can use some time and so can you and I."

Murphy stood. "I'll let them know." He stopped. "What about our assignment with Elizabeth?"

Abe looked up. "That's up in the air right now. Until she agrees to have security back, we're off that. Nathaniel will keep us in the loop, I'm sure."

Murphy smiled. "I'm sure he will."

The next morning, Nathaniel stood at Elizabeth's door, waiting for her to answer. She pulled the door open and stopped

"Nathaniel, you're back. Come in." She stepped back to let him enter, then stepped forward into his hug.

"I missed you, you know." He laid his chin on the top of her head. She fit just right, he thought.

"I missed you, too. Come into the studio. I'm just finishing up for the morning and then I'm free for the rest of the day."

He followed her and then sank into his favourite chair, one where he could sit and watch her silhouetted against the window.

She sat back at the piano and gathered her thoughts. She needed to finish these lyrics today. She prayed for help and then concentrated back on what she had been working on. Soon, she set aside her work and turned to Nathaniel. His head was back and he was asleep. Great, she thought, my lyrics put him to sleep. She gathered her papers and slipped away, sitting down at the computer. She was soon lost in the process of finalizing the work and sending it on to the singer.

She felt hands on her shoulders and leaned back, looking up at him. He smiled.

"Let's get out of here. It looks as if you could use a break."

She spun her chair around and stood. "That I can. I've put in some long hours. When do you leave again?"

He shrugged. "I'm not sure. Abe has called a team meeting for Monday, so I'm around until at least then."

****

So, he was back, was he? He was really going to have to get him out of her life. He was keeping him from getting to her.

Chapter 15

Eddie studied the handout Carrie had given him. Finally, it looked like they were getting somewhere. He needed to get Elizabeth in here to go over the names with him. He headed for the door, intent on finding her.

Elizabeth sat at the table Eddie indicated. He sat beside her.

"This is not going to be easy. What I have here is a list of people, a list of dates, and a list of places. I need you to look through them and tell what you can remember."

She nodded, took a deep breath, said a prayer for strength and guidance, and then picked up the first sheet.

By the time she was through the last one and had told Eddie everything that she could remember, her face was white and drawn. Fatigue marked every move she made. Eddie watched her, then stood.

"Stay here, Elizabeth. I'll be right back."

Eddie tracked down Caleb in the copy room.

"She's been through everything I had so far. She's given me some more, but there's a lot of it she doesn't know about. I'm not sure who we can go to next. She's reluctant to give any names without talking to them, and that she's not willing to do yet."

"Do we have any names at all we can contact?" Caleb's focus was on the copies he had in his hand.

"I have a couple. I'll head out tomorrow and see what I can find out. But from what she's said, they likely don't know they're targets."

"That doesn't surprise me, the way this is going. If we don't have something in the next day or so, we'll have to set it aside until or unless something comes up. We have too many other investigations on the go."

Eddie nodded. "I know. I'll see what I can find out. I don't think she'll be surprised at having to set it aside. She speaks as if that's the way it's always been."

Caleb looked up at that. "Why would you say that?"

"Just an impression I picked up. She says she's talked to other police departments and they just shrugged this off as nuisance calls."

"We know that's not the case." Caleb sighed. "We really don't have a lot to go on, and I'm afraid that he'll make a try at her."

Eddie nodded. "Abe mentioned that they had trouble on their last assignment. He still feels like his team is being set up."

Caleb turned to look at him. "That's odd. Abe's one of the safest men I know. Let him know we'll help him out any way we can." He paused. "Maybe see if Gideon can help with this mess with Elizabeth. He may be able to find out something we're missing, and our people are good."

"I already asked me to stop by. I've had as much material as I can release to him copied. Of course, Elizabeth could pull it all back and hand it to him. There really isn't much that we can keep from him."

"I know. I'm just at a loss right now, Eddie, to suggest a way to go." Caleb sat back. "He's been quiet in the last couple of weeks, hasn't he?"

Eddie thought about that and then nodded. "He has been. Makes me wonder if it was that guy with the restraining order. But then some of the documentation doesn't fit with him."

****

He watched her house. She wasn't leaving it. She should be. She had things she usually did. So why wasn't she coming out? He knew he couldn't get in, he had already tried.

****

Elizabeth stacked the paperwork neatly and sealed it into an envelope. She needed to go to the post office but was at a point where she didn't like to leave her house.

She walked from her office to her back yard. This has to stop, Lord. I need to get my life back and just how do I do that? Please, give me direction. Lead me. I know it's going to be a tough road yet. Protect my friends who want to step into the way. This is something I have to fight through on my own.

She walked her yard for a while, then, determination in each step, she headed for her house. Grabbing her purse and keys, she locked her house and searching the area, seated herself in her car. She stared ahead for a minute, the backed out and headed to find Caleb. They needed to talk and clear the air. And she already knew he wouldn't like what she wanted to do. If he wouldn't or couldn't go along with her plans, then she was on her own. She knew Nathaniel would balk at her plans, and she didn't want to think of what Abe would say. Enough was enough! This was her life and she needed to reclaim it.

Caleb stared at Elizabeth. They had talked and cleared the air of their differences. But what she wanted to do? He shook his head.

"Do you realize what you're setting yourself up for? We can't provide 24/7 protection for you?"

Elizabeth stared at him, then looked at the door as if she was getting ready to walk out. "I know you can't, Caleb. I don't expect anyone to. I need this to end if I am to go on with my life. And I need it to end now."

Caleb sat back and watched the conflicting emotions on her face. "Then, if you feel you need to, let me get our PR lady and you can work with her. I know you well enough to know you've thought and prayed this through. I'm correct?" At her nod, he continued, "Then, let's get this started. What's Nathaniel going to say?"

She looked at him when he said that. "He really doesn't have a choice, now does he? We're friends. Nothing can go forward while I have this over my head. I'm just so tired of it all, Caleb. So much has been taken away from me, no one will ever know just how hard it was been."

"Have you talked to him?" She shook her head. "You need to. Just an observation from a friend? You mean a lot to him. He's the quiet one on Abe's team, keeps everything inside. I see that changing now you're in his life. He's never said much about his early years."

"We've talked, Caleb. I understand where he's

coming from. Now I just need to clue him in on these plans, and I know I'll have a fight on my hands."

"Let Abe know, okay? If it affects Nathaniel, it will affect the whole team."

She stood. "I will. Now, lead me to your PR department and let's get started."

Chapter 16

Nathaniel stared at her. "You're doing what?"

"You heard me. I'm giving a press conference. I have had enough of this guy controlling my life. If you're on board, great. If not, that's too bad. It's going to go ahead, with or without you." She stared at him. "I have to, Nathaniel. I want my life back."

Abe leaned against the wall in her hallway and watched the two. Neither one was backing down. Nathaniel had yet to say anything but Abe could tell he was processing what she had said.

"What are your plans, Elizabeth?" Abe spoke up.

"I have spoken with the police PR officer. I have gone to my lawyer. Together they are working on a draft statement for me. I will read the statement only, taking no questions." She continued to stare at Nathaniel, awaiting his response.

Nathaniel studied her and studied her eyes. She was afraid, he could tell, but determined to move ahead. "Have you thought about how this will affect others?"

"Don't even ask me that, Nathaniel. That is one thing we're taking into consideration. Nothing will be said about anyone else." She threw up her hands. "I might have known you wouldn't be on board." She turned to leave, and he reached for her arm and stopped her.

"I'm not against this, Elizabeth, but I want to make sure you have thought it through thoroughly and that every step is taken to keep you safe."

The three looked up as the door opened, and Jake walked in. He stopped. "Looks like I walked in on something I don't know if I wanted to walk in on."

Abe spoke up. "Elizabeth is working on a press conference to flush out the person responsible. Nathaniel's just not sure that's how she should go."

Jake's eyes traveled to Nathaniel, read his thoughts, and then moved to Abe. Abe's eyes were shuttered but Jake got the quick glance he shot at Nathaniel, then back to Elizabeth.

"Well, Elizabeth, I guess I need to tell you my story." Jake looked at the hat he was holding. "I'm not sure what your story is, but can we go somewhere we can sit?"

Elizabeth nodded and led the way into her studio. She dropped in the chair Murphy preferred and let the men settle themselves down. Nathaniel sat where he could watch her face, eyes not moving from her.

"What's your story, Jake?" Elizabeth wasn't giving up anything. She was too determined to go ahead with this.

"It goes back a long way, Elizabeth. You know I've been in this busy for many years, longer that you have lived. Your Dad and I go back almost to when we both started up. When I was starting up, I had quite a following for a while, not always the best group. They were really rough and tough. In that group, there was one man no one trusted but no one wanted to go up against.

"To make a long story short, he tried to sabotage

our band, he tried to steal our music, our tunes, our lyrics. He would send letters to the press outlining what he thought we were up to. He had us investigated for drug and alcohol smuggling. This was all done anonymously. It took a while, but he finally was caught. It took your Dad and I and the rest of our band standing up, going to the press, and laying out exactly what he was doing. Someone saw it and turned him in."

Jake hesitated as he saw the sorrow cross Elizabeth's face. "I am not saying you should do the same, but if you are determined to do it, let your Dad and I help you. We've been around for a while and know this business better than the police or any security company you could hire."

Elizabeth sat back against the chair and her eyes slid closed. "Dad never mentioned this."

"No, he wouldn't. He didn't want what he went through to taint your success. You can't have told him, though, or he would be all over it."

She shook her head. "No, I never told anyone until the last few weeks. How did you know?"

Jake shrugged. "I guess you could say it was God. He told me to come here today and talk to you."

She rose, hugged him and then walked out. Nathaniel hesitated, then followed her. He wasn't sure if she wanted him with her, but he planned on being at her side as much as he could.

Abe watched them walk away, then turned to Jake. "Okay, Jake, we're going to need to pick your brain for any ideas. Caleb says he pretty much at a loss right now."

Jake stood. "I'm headed off to see Caleb or Eddie

now. I have an idea who it might be, but I want to talk to them first." He turned to look at Abe. "Keep your eye on my girl for me, Abe. She's the daughter I never had. I would hate to see anything happen to her."

Abe watched as Jake walked away. He laid his head back and stared at the ceiling. God, how do we do just that? It is getting so hard to watch out for her, when she does stuff like this. You are in control, not us. Guide us, keep us, help us to show mercy to those we need to. .

Nathaniel stood and once again watched Elizabeth pace her backyard. He finally went and hands on her arms, stopped her.

"Elizabeth, you need to stop. I know you feel like you need to pace, but you'll wear yourself out, to say nothing of your yard."

She glared up at him. "Nathaniel, stop. You're doing it again. Ordering me around." She shrugged away from him and walked to the end of the yard. "I need to pace in order to think. It's not going to be over tomorrow and I need to realize that."

He nodded, then approached her again, stopping about five feet away. "So what's your real feelings on this?"

She stopped, surprised that he would ask. "I'm not even sure any more. It's been so many years. I know I'm tired of it." She looked past him at the house. "I wonder what Jake's real thoughts are. It's almost as if he knew who it was."

Nathaniel reached and pulled her to him. "I don't think he does. He may just be thinking of what he went through." He felt her head shaking. "Why would you think otherwise?"

She shrugged. "I'm not sure of anything any more, but I know there's something he wasn't saying. Maybe he said something to Abe. I hope he goes to Eddie."

He turned her back to the house. "Have they said when your press conference would be?"

She shook her head. "We have to get the statement ready and have my lawyer approve it. Then I want to warn the others involved what's coming. Their names will be left out."

Abe stood on the deck and watched them approach. They both looked at him and noted the grim look on his face.

Elizabeth's steps faltered. "Abe. What happened?"

"It's your Mom. They rushed her to the hospital a while ago. They couldn't reach you so they called me. Where's your phone?"

She ran past him to her office and picked up her phone. Her father's number showed up and she hit redial.

When she got off the phone from him, she turned. "She's okay. She missed a step to the basement and fell. Just bruised. Dad says they're planning on coming back here for a few weeks."

"They're going back to their home on Oak?" She nodded. "I'll take a look at it for them. Given what's going on, we need to make sure it's safe for them."

"Thank you, Abe. Now if you gentleman will excuse me, I need to work." They watched her walk into her studio.

"Abe, what are we going to do with her?"

Abe shook his head. "I don't know, Nathaniel. From the looks of it, I would say it's your problem."

****

He watched as the men left, then turned to study her home. He needed to get in there. He knew she had the information on him that he needed to destroy. But she was too careful.

Chapter 17

Caleb listened as Jake talked, then sat back. "You really think it's him?"

"I do. Think about it, Caleb. He's from this town, he blew his chance, and I know he resented Elizabeth for her talent. She's got what he always wanted and never truly had." Jake studied his hands. "Both her Dad and I tried working with him, but he just didn't have it. He went to the music halls, music producers, you name it. They all turned him away. His lifestyle preceded him."

Caleb nodded. "I remember him. He wasn't very well liked, if I recall. Do you really think he would go this far?"

Jake looked up at Caleb. "He would go this far and further. I would have no doubt that he would be willing to murder someone to get ahead." He pointed at Caleb. "That makes me afraid for Elizabeth."

"He was here at her concert in the church. I saw him but didn't recognize him until now. There was just something about him that raised a red flag." Caleb drew paper towards him. "I'll have him tracked down and brought in."

"You won't find him, Caleb. He's changed his name, if I remember, but I don't know what he changed it to. He could taken a new name now as well."

"Why do you say that?" Caleb was truly puzzled,

and he shouldn't have been.

"Because it's what that family does. I knew his father and he kept changing their names. Even the name you know him by probably isn't the right one."

Caleb drew a deep breath. "This is when I need Ben Johnson still to be on the force. He knew so many in the town."

"Go talk with him or send Eddie or Frankie."

"I wish I could. He and Marg are out of town an extended vacation. I don't know where they are, though Timothy might."

"Talk to him or Frankie might. Deirdre may have said." Jake knew Deidre, Ben's niece an Frankie's wife, and Timothy, Ben's son, by sight. He stood to leave. "If I come up with anything else, I'll call."

"Thanks, Jake. This is a start."

Jake nodded. "I know this is why cases go cold, you run out of information, clues, what have you. I just don't want that to happen to Elizabeth."

"I don't either, Jake, but right now, that's the way this is headed."

The day of her statement dawned bright and sunny, not a cloud in the sky. Elizabeth stood at the podium, reading her prepared statement, laying out the facts as she had them, cameras flashing at her and the TV stations with their video cameras rolling. Her voice was steady and calm, belying the nerves she felt. When she was finished, she stepped back, ignoring the calls and questions. Her part was done.

Nathaniel had been standing behind her and stepped forward to come between her and the cameras. He turned her towards the door of the police department.

Joseph and Micah were beside him when Joseph saw a small red flash. He shoved them forward and down, going down himself. Micah went the other way, eyes above the crowd, searching. They had a sniper. Mica

h flinched as a chunk of concrete block flew at his face Nathaniel shoved Elizabeth through the door as the officers surrounding them reacted. The crowd scattered with screams and shouts. Police officers responded, weapons drawn as they raced across the road, searching for the perpetrator.

Elizabeth spun as they caught their balance. "What was that all about?" Her eyes were wide and scared.

"Sniper."

"A sniper?" She shook her head. "He wouldn't go that far."

"You think? You put yourself out there as a target, listing what he's done, and you don't think he would go this far?" Nathaniel was angry, not so much at her as at the one she was trying to draw out.

Elizabeth stared past him as Micah entered, blood dripping from the scratch on his face. "Micah! Your face!"

He shrugged as he swiped at it with his jacket sleeve. "It's nothing. Don't look at me like that." He turned to Nathaniel. "I take it you figured out it was a sniper?"

"I did. We shouldn't have had her out there."

Micah held up his hand. "You see, Nathaniel, there's a slight problem with that. She wasn't the target. You were."

Nathaniel spun to stare at his team mate. "What do you mean? I should have no one after me!"

"But you do. The bullet was aimed too high for Elizabeth. It was aimed at your head. He meant to kill you today."

Elizabeth gasped. "Nathaniel!"

Nathaniel reached for her and gathered her under his arm. "He missed. Then how did he miss?"

"Joseph moved you in time. If he hadn't seen the red flash, we wouldn't be having this conversation." He turned to look back out the window of the door, at the scattering of the people, and the flashing of police lights. "I don't think they're going to find him. He'll be long gone."

Joseph stepped in behind Micah and then motioned for them to move further into the building. "We need to get you two out of here. Abe wants you at Rebel's yesterday. The vehicle's at the back door. Let's move."

Elizabeth and Nathaniel were shoved into the vehicle. Joseph carefully wended his way through the crowd and once free headed as fast as he could for Rebel's. Micah's eyes never stopped moving as he searched around them. Nathaniel's eyes were on the move as well, seeking for the one who had tried to kill him.

Abe stood and watched as Nathaniel and Elizabeth walked up the steps to his house. He jerked his head to the door. Elizabeth glared at him and he had to hide a smile. She was feisty again. That's what had been missing for the last few weeks.

Abe shut the door behind them and then turned to

them, indicating the living room. Elizabeth plopped herself down, without saying anything.

Nathaniel paced back and forth from hallway to window. He couldn't settle down. Who had tried to take him out? He had no enemies that he knew of.

"Nathaniel, sit." Abe stared at him until he did. "I've talked to Caleb. You were definitely the target. We just need to figure out why and who."

"I don't get it, Caleb. There's nothing in my past, other than this job, that would warrant anyone going after me. You've met my family. There is just nothing there."

Abe nodded. "I know. That's what I told Caleb. He'll need to investigate that on his own." He paused before he continued. "I agree. I think it's the team. It could be Elizabeth and someone wanted to take you out to get to her. That's something else we have to consider."

Elizabeth jumped to her feet. "I wish I had never come back here." She moved to go past Abe and he stopped her.

"It wouldn't have mattered, Elizabeth. The timing of this is that he would have gone after you anywhere you went. Here, you're among friends. Let us help you. This time, I'm asking, not telling." A faint smile crossed his face. He wasn't sure how she would react.

She paused, then turned back to sit once again. "I know that, Abe. I just wish I didn't. Why couldn't he have picked someone else?"

"I think you have an idea who it is." Abe sat on the coffee table in front of her. "Jake mentioned a name. Tell me who you think it is."

She shook her head.

"Elizabeth, keeping quiet is not helping. You need to give us what you know as well as what you're guessing. Your guess might just be right."

She sighed as she stared past time, distress on her face and hurt in her eyes. "I don't know, Abe. I really don't know who it would be. There is Terry Adams. He thought he was so good but his attitude really destroyed his relationships with people. He tried to con Mrs. C. but she read him better than anyone. Other than him, he's the only one I can think of."

"That's a name that we can work with." Abe reached for her hands and rubbed them to warm them. "If you think of others, you need to let us know." He turned to Nathaniel. "We'll need to meet as a team, Nathaniel. I have Micah working on tracking through our assignments, to see if he can find a pattern. There's something there, somewhere."

"Someone's been after you, Abe, for a while. We need to look at that as well." Nathaniel stared out the window from where he sat. "The last few times, I've felt like we were being set up."

"So do the others. Murphy is going over the next few assignments we're to go on. He has Gideon and Sidney doing background research." Gideon, Abe's brother-in-law, ran an investigative firm and his former employer, Sidney, often gave a hand with research.

Elizabeth drew her knees up and wrapped her arms around them, fatigue radiating from her. She rested her chin on her knees and contemplated the two men. "All I wanted was to be free of this monster. Now, it sounds like I am involved in something a whole lot deeper.”

“I hope not, Elizabeth, I hope not.” Abe stood, hesitated, and then walked towards the door. “For now, it would please me if you chose to stay here, Elizabeth, but it is your decision. Rebecca won’t mind if you raid her closet for some casual clothes.” Abe walked away from them.

Chapter 18

Nathaniel approached Abe later that day with questions he knew could not be answered.

"Where do we go from here, Abe? We can't stay locked up forever."

Abe sat back in his chair. "I know we can't. It's the uncertainty of when he will strike next. It's disturbing, that sniper this morning."

Nathaniel watched as Abe mulled over the morning's incident. "You really think he was after me?"

Abe nodded. "From what I've been told, he was. Now, as to why, that's a good question."

Nathaniel shook his head as he rose. "Elizabeth won't stay here, you know. She's wanting to go home tomorrow."

Abe sighed. "I know. And we can't make her stay." He looked up at Nathaniel. "We've got some pretty heavy duty commitments and training coming up. I need your head on straight and you with us totally."

Nathaniel looked back at him. "It will be. I have had to learn to set aside personal stuff and concentrate."

"You never talk much about your family."

"None of us do, for some reason. I'm the middle one, two older brothers, two younger sisters. I had to be the peacemaker and stay calm, cool and collected."

A small smile appeared.

"That's what makes you good at your job. Thankfully, we've never had to use your talents yet."

"And I pray we never do." Nathaniel walked away on that, leaving Abe staring after him.

****

He had the room already for him. He just had to find him when he was on his own. Somehow he would do that. He was watching and waiting. Once he had Nathaniel in his control, getting to Elizabeth would be easy. She would do anything for her friends.

****

It had been a month since she gave her news conference. Elizabeth wandered through her house. There had been no more contact from him. She was scared. She felt like there was more to come and he was just waiting for the opportune time. When would it end and she would be free?

She stopped at her desk and reached for the song sheets she was to be working on. Inspiration was dry today. It happened every once in a while. She needed to get out and do something different. That was it, she thought, as she reached for her car keys. I'll go see May.

May looked up as Elizabeth entered her tea room. It was empty for the moment.

"Elizabeth, welcome. What brings you here today?"

"I just needed to talk to someone other than a guy. All my women friends are busy. I consider you my friend. Up for some girl talk?"

May laughed. "Always, dear. You look so much like your mother now. When are they coming back?"

"Dad figures in the next couple of weeks they'll be around to get things organized and set up at the house. They plan to move back in about six weeks or so. I miss them.'

May reached for Elizabeth and drew her to the piano. "I know you do. Facing what you have on your own has not been easy. Trying to scare him out of hiding has to have been terrifying for you. Here. Sit. Play for me like you used to. I'll even take your version of Chopsticks."

Elizabeth laughed. "Will no one ever forget that?"

May shook her head. "It was just so you, what you did. Mrs. C. told me afterwards she knew better than to put you on the spot. Even though she hasn't said anything, she is proud of you and what you have accomplished. She also realizes your talent is from God. She felt bad that she tried to push you in a different direction all those years ago."

"Sounds like I need to go find her at some point."

"She would like to see you. She asks about you when she's in. Don't wait too long though. She's not well."

Elizabeth's eyes raised to May's and read the message. "I'll go this week, May."

Nathaniel stood at Elizabeth's door and looked around. She couldn't be home, he thought. Now where would he find her? He watched as a small car slowly drove by, his eyes narrowing as he watched. It was driving too slow for his liking, almost as if the driver was searching for a house number. He shrugged off his uneasiness.

Heading back towards Rebel's, he slowed and pulled off into the park's lot. He needed some time with God, and being out in the open always helped. He locked his truck and moved away, not seeing or hearing the car pull in behind him.

The man stood by his car and watched Nathaniel head out on one of the paths. Perfect, he thought. Now I have my opportunity. Soon, Elizabeth, soon you will be in my hands and pay for what you have cost me.

"Have you seen Nathaniel?" Abe stuck his head into Micah's cottage.

"No, I haven't, not since the morning. He was headed to Elizabeth's and he said he'd be back by 4."

"And it's now 6." Abe fished his phone out of his pocket and searched for the number he wanted.

"Lyrics by Whizz. Elizabeth speaking."

"Elizabeth, it's Abe."

"Abe! When did you guys get back? This afternoon?" He could hear the suppressed joy in her voice and knew she was hoping to see Nathaniel.

"Actually, we got in late last night. Have you seen Nathaniel?"

"No." He could hear the hesitation in her voice. "I was out for a while today, so if he stopped by, I wouldn't have known. And I didn't get any messages from him." She stopped speaking. "Oh, Abe! You don't think."

"Right now, I'm hoping it's just his vehicle broken down. Let me call you back."

Micah was on his feet and moving for the door as Abe clicked off his phone from Elizabeth and then dialled the police station. Abe was giving details as the rest of his team found him.

"Nathaniel's missing. Elizabeth hasn't seen or heard from him and we know that's where he would have been heading." Abe paced, deep in thought. "Where would he go if he wanted to think, or be by himself?"

Murphy spoke up. "I don't think he's really ever said. He's quiet about what he does when he's off site."

Micah, who knew him best of the team, agreed. "I know he likes to spend time outdoors but exactly where I'm not sure. Come to think of it, a while ago, he said he and Elizabeth had spent some time wandering some nature paths he liked to follow." Micah was on the phone with Elizabeth, confirming a location for where they had been and was then reaching for a topographical map of the area.

"She says in this area. It's a large area to search."

Abe nodded grimly. "And we're coming up to nightfall. Joseph, you and Murphy head for there. See if his truck's there first."

Chapter 19

Nathaniel rolled to his side, his stomach roiling as he did so. He kept his eyes closed, hoping that it would help. He could hear nothing, see nothing when he opened his eyes. It was completely black. Where was he? The last he remembered was hiking back to his truck.

The man stood in the doorway and watched, snickering to himself. It was so easy to take Nathaniel down. A little prick with a dart and he was on the ground. Now he had to think of how to get Elizabeth to come to him. With her boyfriend gone, they would be extra vigilant. He closed the door with a quiet sound and locked it. There was no way out of that room but through that door and he had done his best to make sure it was solid and secure.

****

Elizabeth sat in Caleb's office, her face white and strained, and watched the activity going on around her. Nathaniel was missing and had been for most of the day. Joseph and Murphy hadn't found his truck, had found no evidence that he had been at the hiking trails.

Caleb stood just outside his office door and studied her. He knew she was near the breaking point and he was afraid this would be enough to send her over the edge. He listened to the conversation going on around him. They just had so many investigations ongoing at the moment. Right now, Nathaniel's disappearance took priority, having already been the target of a sniper.

"Where do we stand right now?"

Eddie shook his head. "Right now, no where. We have no idea where he is. It's like he decided just to climb in his truck and drive out of town and keep going."

Caleb turned keen eyes on Eddie. "That's exactly what we're to think. So that means it must be here in town somewhere. Have Frankie hit the streets and his sources."

"He's already on it. He's hoping someone heard or knows something. This has just seemed so off and so wrong from day one." Eddie stepped back so he could look at Elizabeth. "She's the target, but I think Abe is as well, given what happened with Matt."

Caleb nodded. "I know and that worries me. We have no idea who would be after Abe. There are just too many people who might want a piece of him."

Elizabeth jumped as Micah handed her a bottle of juice. "Thank you." Her voice was quieter than normal.

"How are you doing?" Micah was concerned about her, she was just too quiet.

She tilted her head back and looked up at him and then shrugged. "Right now, Micah, I couldn't tell you how I feel. It's just so overwhelming."

He nodded and then sat down in the chair beside her. "One thing I do know. You and Nathaniel have great faith and trust in God. Keep your eyes on Him. We're all praying."

She looked over at him as she took a swig of juice.

"You never used to feel that way. I got the vibes at the beginning. You all resented me."

He smiled. "Maybe a bit but that was before we got to know you. You see, we provide security for "VIPs", and these people usually are rude, inconsiderate, and intolerant. To them, we're just like a piece of furniture. To be asked to provide security on short notice for a celebrity really threw us. We had no idea what to expect. You've proved yourself to us, even though you didn't have to. When Nathaniel told Abe and Caleb off, the respect for you went way up. Nathaniel is our calm, cool, and collected one. He has to be to have his position on the team. He's not a hot head. So when he told those two off, we knew he had read something in you we missed. That respect for him transferred to you."

She reached for his hand and squeezed it. "Thank you, Micah. I wondered. I could feel the change in them towards me and never knew why." She looked around the office. "Now, I need to get out of here and I don't think I'm going to be able to. Will you help me?"

Micah shook his head. "No, we need you to stay right here. Abe will handcuff you to that chair if you try to leave." He smiled as he said that but she knew he meant it.

She sat back heavily. "All right, then. Now, I need to see Jake. Can you arrange for him to come here? He knows the woods around here better than anyone I can think off. He may have an idea. If you think Nathaniel is being held outside of town." She paused as she thought, and then her face whitened even more. "Oh no, Micah. I just thought of a place and I hope he's not there."

Micah reached for her as she slid forward. It was not like her to faint. Caleb turned at his quiet call, and then sent Eddie for Matt. Micah laid her on the couch and then stepped back as Matt knelt beside her.

"She's worn out, Caleb. I don't think she can take much more of this. I doubt she's been eating properly either." Matt turned to Caleb. "We need to get her to the hospital where she can be assessed and rehydrated."

Elizabeth had roused as Matt spoke. "No. No hospital. I won't go."

Caleb stood over her. "Elizabeth, you need help and that help is in the hospital."

She shook her head. "Call Paul Owens. He'll bring what you need. He has that free clinic down town." Her eyes slid closed and she slipped away from them again.

Caleb looked up as Abe entered his office. "Did you hear?"

Abe nodded. "I made the call to Paul. He'll grab what he needs and head in." He watched as Matt continued to care for Elizabeth. "What happened?"

"We have no idea. She was talking with Micah and then fainted. I don't remember her ever fainting in all the time we've known her."

"No, she never has that we're aware of." His speech broke off as he turned with the new commotion in the entry. "There's Jake, and there's her father. When did he get here?"

Paul Owens sat back on his heels and turned to Elizabeth's father. "Aaron, what is going on with her? She shouldn't be like this. It's like she's been starving herself or something."

Aaron Steele nodded. "I think she has been. She hasn't said anything to us, but whatever's been going on has weighed heavily on her. She asked us about prayer and fasting a couple of weeks ago. We told her what we knew, but we also stressed that she not do it without medical approval."

Paul looked back at Elizabeth. "I would say that's what she's been doing, but the stress she's been under should have precluded her from fasting. Obviously she didn't get medical advice."

"No, I think she did. I just don't think she's really thinking straight. This whole thing has consumed her in the last few weeks. She's desperate to have it over with." He looked back at his daughter. "What do you suggest?"

"What I suggest is that we move her to the hospital, but she is adamant she's not going there. The next best thing is to find somewhere we can monitor her care. She's going to need to be on IV for a few days. That we can do at home with a nurse supervising it. I have someone I know who would be willing to step in. Caleb, Abe, find somewhere safe for her."

"That's the million dollar question, Paul." Caleb turned and studied the area outside his office. "Word's going to get out that she collapsed. We can't keep it quiet."

"Then we use it to our advantage." Jake spoke up. "Use it to draw him out. This guy, whoever he is, likely has Nathaniel and will use him to draw her out and to him. Use this to draw him out. He won't hurt Nathaniel if he thinks he can use him to get to Elizabeth. That's how these guys think."

Aaron Steele spoke up. "I have a pretty good idea who it is." He said a name and the eyes of the other men flew to his. "That's who you need to find. Unfortunately, he's a master at disguise. Always has been. A lot of what went on when you were all teenagers was traced back to him but without real proof, no one could charge him. I want him now for what he's done to my daughter." He turned to Caleb. "Have someone write up a statement for me and I'll read it."

His statement read, Aaron returned to Caleb's office. Plans were in place and they were ready to move Elizabeth. Aaron stood by his daughter, sorrow lacing through him at what she had suffered for so long in silence. It would change, he thought. Lord, protect her friend. Bring him back safely.

Chapter 20

No, he thought, they wouldn't do that to him. He was so close to getting her in his grasp. Why did she have to go and get sick? Now they were putting her somewhere he had no idea where. He spun in rage and sent the chair he had been sitting on flying across the room, to land broken on the floor. This meant he would have to hold on to her boyfriend for longer than he planned, and that was not a good thing.

****

Nathaniel stirred at the crash of the chair. It was still pitch dark. His eyes opened and stayed open this time. He pushed himself to a sitting position. How long had he been in here, he wondered? And just where was here? He struggled to his feet and found the wall behind him, tracing his way by feel around the room. It was small, he thought, with no window and only the door to get in and out of. He reached for the ceiling. Tile he thought but likely a wood floor right above that. He slumped back to the floor, exhausted. How, dear Lord, are You going to get me out of this mess? Did I really need to spend time alone with You this bad?

Aaron closed the door to his daughter's room. Abe had opened his home to them. With Matt on site, it just made sense, Aaron thought. He walked heavily out to the kitchen and sank into a chair at the table.

Abe set a cup of coffee in front of him and then sat

across from him.

"Tell me, Abe, tell me what all has been going on. She hasn't said a word in all these years."

Abe looked with compassion at his friend and then detailed what all he knew. "There's more that I don't know. Caleb or Eddie or even Frankie would be the ones to tell you what they can." He studied his folded hands. "Aaron, can I ask you something?"

"Go ahead, Abe. You know you can."

"I can remember years ago when something happened, and I can't even remember what it was now, you spoke to us about having mercy on someone. That it was God who should avenge, not us." He paused, unable to continue for a moment. "How do you extend mercy to someone like this?"

Aaron studied his coffee cup for a few minutes, then looked at Abe. "How much do we deserve God's mercy? How much mercy does He extend to us? We don't deserve it. He has given it freely. Well, not quite freely. Christ had to die on the cross for that. But He expects us to forgive those who have harmed us. Part of forgiveness is extending mercy to them." He paused, rose to refill his coffee cup and sat back down.

"When I was a teenager, I had problems with another youth. It was to the point we were into fist fights and what have you. My Dad pulled me aside one day and sat me down. He explained to me what was going on with the other youth and that as a Christian, I needed to show God's love and mercy towards him. It took a while but I listened to my father." He paused to smile. "If I hadn't, I would have lost someone who has become almost like a brother to me."

Abe's eyes were questioning him. "Who?"

"Jake. We didn't see things the same way when we were young, but after Dad spoke with me and then set both of us down together, we worked it through. Who hurt you that bad, Abe?"

Abe shook his head and got up and walked away. He couldn't speak of the hurt he had been dealt. Even all those years later, it still felt raw.

Elizabeth stirred, moving slightly. She opened her eyes and squinted. It was night, she could tell. A low light burned on the table by her bed. She raised herself up. No, it wasn't her bedroom. Where was she? She willed the rising panic back down and looked around again. No, she didn't know this room. She swung her legs over the side of the bed and felt a pull on her arm. An IV, she thought. Okay, so what's going on?

A tap came at the door and then the door cracked open. Matt peeked in and seeing her sitting up, came in.

"Where am I, Matt?"

"At Abe's. Your Dad thought it was the best place for you."

"Dad. He's here?"

Matt nodded. "Jake had gone to get him. He said your Mom is flying in tomorrow or the next day." He reached to check her IV. "I'll pull the IV, Elizabeth, but if I think it needs to go back in it will. You fainted on us yesterday."

"I don't faint." Her tone was disgruntled.

Matt gave a low laugh. "Nathaniel said you had a

list of things you don't do. We'll add that to the list."
He patted a bandage into place of her arm.

"Nathaniel." Her eyes flew to his. "Any word?"

"Nothing yet. It's like he's disappeared into thin air."

"I wish I knew where he was." She wrapped her arms around herself. "God knows. Why is He keeping it from us?"

Matt crouched in front of her. "I don't know, Elizabeth. That's where trust comes in and before you say you don't do trust, think about it. God is working through this."

She nodded. "I know." A yawn caught her unawares. "I think I need to go back to sleep."

Matt grinned. "I think you do." He watched as she settled back down and drew the covers up over herself, then turned and walked from the room. He stopped, looked up, a question in his heart.

A sound at the door roused Nathaniel. He had no idea as to time of day or even what day it was. A light blinded him, and then a muffled voice spoke.

"Stand up." When he didn't stand, the command was repeated.

He struggled to his feet, balancing himself on the wall. He was ordered to walk forward, following the light as it backed away. He was roughly shoved down a hall and into another room, this time with a small window. The door clicked behind him. He turned and surveyed the room. At least, there was a bed and chair and light. It would take a while for him to get used to the light again.

He walked towards the bed and noticed for the first

time the paper on it. He picked it up, staring around the room.

Your girlfriend is playing with me and I don't like that. She needs to stop her press conferences, her fake illness, her bringing in her daddy to help. I will be back and you WILL help me to reach her.

Nathaniel sank to the floor, the paper shaking in his hand. He read it again. No, he would not help this maniac, whoever he was. He would refuse. There was no way he would draw Elizabeth into something like this, to where she could be harmed.

But what did he mean about fake illness? If he only knew she was okay.

Caleb stared at the white board in the conference room. They had one name but so many aliases for him. How did they ever find him?

Eddie stood watching Caleb, seeing the strain in his face, his stance. He walked towards him, touched his arm, and told him to go home. Caleb nodded, knowing they were at a standstill.

Chapter 21

Abe looked up as Jake and Aaron entered his office and then sat.

"We have a suggestion to make, Abe." Aaron was hesitant to speak. "I know how stretched the police resources are and I know that Gideon would be helping if he could be here instead of away on that court case. I have a friend who runs a tracking business, specifically to find people like this man. I put a call into her and she's sending one of her men over to talk with us. I'm not interfering with the police investigation. We just need to expand how we're searching."

"That's fine, Aaron. It's your daughter who's involved. I would be doing the same." Abe sat back. "Now about this company? You know the woman who runs it?"

"I do. And I know the men and women she has working for her. They're the best in what they do. Tracker will help."

"Tracker? That's her name?"

Jake looked at Aaron, then spoke. "It's the name she's known by. She refuses to give any other name. People who know her respect her wishes. Clients who push are politely steered elsewhere."

Abe shrugged. "It doesn't really matter, as long as they can help. How long before he can be here?"

"Tracker has her office just outside of town, on the

other side from you. She has someone free and was sending him over, Jace Taylor she called him."

The two older men stood. "Let us know when he gets here. He was told to ask for you."

Abe looked down at the paperwork he had been ensconced in, then looked at his computer. Sighing, he gave in to his impulse and searched for the company, Tracker. Finding their website, he searched but could find no list of any employee names or even the owner's name. He read through what was there. She's careful, Tracker is, he thought. Must be the kind of business she's in that makes her that way.

A knock at his door had him on his feet. He assessed the man who stood in the doorway. Dark hair, glasses, 5'7" maybe. His assessment was quick and he knew he was being assessed as well.

"You're Jace Taylor?"

Jace nodded, reached to shake his hand, and then handed him a business card. "Tracker asked me to see if I could help. She thinks a lot of Aaron and Jake. So tell me what you can?"

"Have a seat. It will take a while, and I'm thinking I'll have to take you in to see either Eddie or Frankie at the police department."

Jace nodded and pulled out a portfolio and pen. He laughed at Abe's quick look of surprise. "Old-fashioned ways still work."

Deeply engrossed in discussing the case, they barely heard or saw Jake and Aaron slip back in and sit.

Jace finally sat back. "All I can say is Wow! How did she ever keep it a secret?"

Aaron spoke up. "That's Elizabeth. If she doesn't want you to know something, she doesn't tell you. The only thing she did tell me once was that a friend was being stalked and harassed about the song she was planning on releasing, and that another friend has being harassed. She never gave names or went back to explain any further."

Jace nodded. "Okay, so what I need now is a list of her friends and contacts here in town." He looked up as the men laughed. "I take it she has a lot?"

Jake smiled. "She can make a friend in a minute, but true deep friendship takes a lot longer. Abe knows. He's been a friend for years. I would suggest you also talk to her music teacher, Mrs. C., and also May at the tearoom. She spends time with them when she can."

Jace nodded. "I think I have what I need for now. Let me get running with this. I should have a preliminary report late tonight or tomorrow afternoon."

"That soon?" Abe couldn't help but question him.

Jace smiled. "We're good at what we do, Abe. Tracker has streamlined how we work so that there is very little time or effort wasted."

They watched him walk away. "I hope he can find something we can't."

"Trust me, Abe, he will." Aaron rose to go and find his daughter. He knew she had been up and around and that Matt was making her eat, much to her dismay.

Jake watched Abe. "There's something bugging you, Abe. What is it?"

Abe just shook his head. "Nothing you can help

with, Jake, thanks. It's personal."

"If you need to talk, come find me."

****

He slammed the door to the house, the sound echoing through. They had brought in someone new. How dare they! Did they not realize that he would do away with Nathaniel before he let him be found! He snatched at the bag of food he had picked up, pulled on his mask, and headed for the room Nathaniel was locked in. Opening the door, he stared at him, eyes narrowed in hatred.

Nathaniel sat on the edge of the bed, calmly watching his captor. He saw the bag of food and knew he needed desperately to eat. The food was set on the floor and his captor backed away, locking the door behind him. When would he be ready for Nathaniel to play his part? And Nathaniel already had his part to play mapped out, and it didn't include sending a message to Elizabeth to lure her away from her safety team.

****

Caleb looked up as Frankie entered his office and handed him a file.

"Just had one of Tracker's men in. Jake and Aaron called her."

"Which one?"

"Jace. He's one of her best. He's hoping he might have some information by tomorrow at the latest."

"It wouldn't surprise me if he did. She's trained them well." Caleb sat back. "Have you ever met her?"

Eddie shook his head. "Once or twice. Have

you?"

"No, but I would like to. She doesn't often make it in to town, or at least, not that I know of. She keeps to herself. Someone must have really hurt her bad in the past for her to be like this."

Eddie studied the floor, not sure how to respond. "I got that impression from Jace, that she wants to help people, but won't take help herself." He sighed. "I just hope they find our guy."

"She has an interesting approach to tracking people down. She finds them, gives the information to the client, and then steps away from them. It's up to the client to follow up with what she's dug up."

Eddie was surprised. "I didn't know that. That's one way to do business."

"And if the person is found and doesn't want anything to do with their client, the client is told that the person is alive and well and that their whereabouts are not disclosed at the person's request. She has been threatened a few times but she has an iron-clad contract." He looked at the door as one of the officers appeared.

"Caleb, I think you need to see this." He was handed an envelope. "We've gone over it. It's clean."

Caleb reached for it and pulled out the piece of paper inside. His heart sank. They knew now that Nathaniel was not missing, he had been kidnapped. But why? Was it Elizabeth or was it Abe?

Eddie rose to read over Caleb's shoulder and shuddered.

"This guy is sick. Does he think Elizabeth will come forward and meet him, while he's threatening

Nathaniel?"

Caleb read through the note again. "He does. And I'm afraid that's just what she will do." He handed Eddie the note. "Where do we go from here? I'm at a loss. We know who this guy is but we can't find him no matter how hard we're digging. Gideon and Sidney haven't come up with anything either."

They looked up at a tap on the door.

"Jace, you just left not that long ago." Caleb beckoned him in.

Jace handed him a slip of paper. "He was there 30 minutes ago, long enough to take in a bag of food, but not long enough to have stayed and eaten it himself. I have a good idea where he's headed next."

"How did you do this so quick?" Caleb was astonished.

"Easy. I went by Elizabeth's house and waited. When the car I knew he had been using drove by, I followed him."

"And how did you know what car he was driving?" Eddie was frustrated that Jace had found something they had missed.

"Not as easy as you think, Eddie. I had Tracker and Naomi run aliases and likely makes and models. We got lucky with one."

"No, not luck." Caleb was quick to speak up.

"No, God did it."

"Let's get a warrant, Eddie. We should have enough for probable cause for entering a kidnapper's house. Let's hope he hasn't been moved in the meanwhile."

"I would know if he had. I have someone

watching the house."

"Well, at least that's a bit of good news. Care to share who?"

Jace shook his head. "That's not how we work."

Chapter 22

Caleb stood on the sidewalk, watching the house as the ETF team prepared to enter. He prayed Nathaniel was here. Hearing a motor, he turned and watched a black truck pull away from the curb down the street aways and drive off. His eyes narrowed and then he nodded. That would have been whoever Jace said was watching.

He turned as Doug came back towards him.

"We have Nathaniel, Caleb. It looks as if he's been drugged, but other than that, I think he's okay. I'm sending in the paramedics to get him and then we're turning the house over to the evidence team." He turned to study the house. "I don't think we'll find much though. The house looks clean."

Caleb breathed a sigh of relief. "At least we have him." He walked towards the house with Doug. "You say the house is clean?"

Doug nodded. "It's like it's a brand new house, never been lived in. No furniture except where Nathaniel is. Very strange."

Caleb stepped through the front door and saw what Doug meant. "We'll need to track down the owners of this house and see what's going on. Where is Nathaniel?"

"In a room at the back. There's also a room in the centre of the house that looks as if he was there for a while." Doug looked around. "I just don't get it."

Caleb shook his head, then watched as the paramedics wheeled the stretcher carrying Nathaniel by him. "I don't either. I'll be at the hospital if you need me."

Abe shook the sleep from his head and picked up his phone. "Caleb, what's up?"

"We've found Nathaniel. I'm at the hospital with him right now. He's been drugged, so I haven't been able to speak with him."

Abe reached for his clothes. "I'm on my way."

Heading down the stairs, he saw a light in the kitchen and headed that way. Jake sat at the table, paper in front of him.

"They've found Nathaniel, Jake. I'm headed to the hospital."

Jake looked up, a smile on his face. "I knew they would. Let us know how he is. I'll try and keep Elizabeth here but once she knows where he is, I'm not sure I can."

"Do your best. I'll call when I find out more. Let me have your number."

Caleb turned as Abe strode rapidly towards him across the parking lot.

"What's the word, Caleb?"

"It's what we suspected. He was sedated and not just once. The doctors think it'll be at least 24 hours before he's alert enough they can send him home. We won't be able to talk with him much before tomorrow afternoon, they think."

Abe drew a deep breath. "You know my guys are going to want to be on security detail for him. How do I keep them away?"

"We don't. We work together on security for him. We just can't let Elizabeth know where he is until we can get him back to your place."

"Now that I want to see you try. Jake said the same thing."

Caleb turned to re-enter the hospital, Abe at his side. "Talk to him and her Dad. See what we can do about that. I don't want her out there until we find this guy."

****

He pulled to a stop near the house and watching the activity. How did they find him? He pounded the steering wheel in frustration. Now how was he to get to her? He peeled away from the curb, leaving rubber on the pavement, not caring if he was heard. They didn't know his vehicle, couldn't see it in the dark.

****

Elizabeth looked up from where she was sitting. Abe stood in the doorway, a shuttered look on his face. Her face paling, she started shaking her head, afraid of what he had to say.

Abe sat on the coffee table in front of her and reached for her hands. "It's okay, Whizz. We have Nathaniel. Matt's getting him settled in his cottage right now. I'll take you out to him later."

Her eyes slid closed. Thank you, Lord, for bringing him back. Eyes popping open again, she stared at Abe. "Where was he and what happened?"

"Your dad and Jake called in a friend by the name of Tracker and she sent Jace. You know them?" At her nod, he continued, "They're good. Jace was by your house, followed a vehicle with a plate number they suspected right to where Nathaniel was being held. Caleb got the warrants and they found him. He's been drugged, so it's taking a while for him to rouse."

"When did they find him?"

"When?"

She nodded. "Yes, when. What time?"

"I don't know. It was sometime after midnight, before 2, I think."

She nodded once again. "That's when I had peace that he would be found. I'm okay, Abe. Go, do what you need to. Come get me when I can see him."

Abe stared at her, then shook his head. "You never fail to amaze me, Whizz. Here, I thought you'd be really upset, and you're calm and peaceful."

She just smiled. "That I am." Her eyes dropped back to her book and she dismissed him.

Abe stood for a moment, then went to find Matt.

Caleb stood in the conference room. How had they missed the fact he had more than one house to his name? They really dropped the ball on that one, he thought.

"Listen up, people. We need to dig a lot deeper and into more areas than we have been. A private company that is really good a research found what we missed, in less than two hours. Don't let them show us up again, okay?"

He turned and walked from the room back to his office. He turned as he heard his name. He didn't know the woman approaching him.

"Can we talk somewhere outside of here?" She handed him her card.

He glanced at it, then at her. "Sure. Just let me

grab my jacket."

They walked towards the town square and sat on one of the benches.

"So, you're Tracker?" At her nod, he hesitated, noting that she offered no other name. "Thanks for finding Nathaniel for us."

"That's what we do, Caleb. We're dedicated to finding people. We work with the law, not outside of it. My people are highly trained."

"I can see that." He waited a minute, then continued, "But that's not why you're here, what happened last night?"

She shook her head and handed him a folder she had been carrying. "No, it's part of last night. Here's the information you'll need to find this fellow, but he's a chameleon, changing appearance, addresses, vehicles at a whim. It's like he thinks he's in a movie or something. But there's more." She stopped to gather her thoughts.

"When Naomi was researching this, she found some threats against the company Nathaniel works for. I haven't read them. Naomi is one of my best researchers. If she says they're real, they are. You need to pass them on to the owner."

"You could do that." Caleb waited for her response.

"No, I wouldn't be the one doing that. Whoever is the one doing the research for me, that's who they talk to. That way nothing is lost between what they found and what is told. The same for last night. Naomi is the one who pretty much ran the research. She bounced ideas off me but it was her task. She's the one Jace called. Talk to her. Have her talk to your people. Just keep me out of it, please."

Caleb watched as she kept a tight control on her face. "I will. But let me help you too."

She shook her head and stood. "There's not much one can do for me now, Caleb. What happened in the past is why I set up Tracker's."

He watched as she turned and walked away, tall, slender, in control, red hair that made him think of the dark red of turning maple leaves, and slate gray eyes. Lord, this lady's hurting. Heal her. I wish I could take her to Hannah. Hannah, my wife, has such a way with those hurting.

He then rose and headed for his vehicle. He needed to find Abe.

Chapter 23

Abe watched as Matt helped Nathaniel to the couch. There would be no way Nathaniel would be out on their assignments for a while. Caleb had tapped at the door and entered.

"Nathaniel, can you remember anything?" Caleb was pushing and everyone knew it.

"Not a thing. I can remember looking for Elizabeth and then heading out on one of the trails. I was almost at my truck and went down. I don't remember much after that, other than being in a room that was totally dark, and then being moved to a room with a small window." Even just that much talking had exhausted him. "Was it him?"

"We're sure it was. We figure he went after you to get to Elizabeth."

"Please tell me you got him."

"No, I'm sorry, Nathaniel. We didn't, but we've been given more information from a tracking/research firm. That's how we found you last night. They tracked him down but the researcher says he's a master at disguise." He handed Abe a folder. "This is what he came up with. I got word the car was found abandoned and wiped clean."

"So, we're really not any better off than we were before." Abe was growing frustrated. "Where do we go from here, Caleb? Has the investigation stalled that badly?"

"It had but wth this new information, I'm hoping it moves ahead. There's something else, Abe. I need to talk to you and you'll need to talk to your guys afterwards. Nathaniel, if you think of anything let me know."

Nathaniel nodded wearily, eyes closed. He felt like he had been run over by a Mack truck.

Abe turned to Caleb once they were outside. "Okay, so what's got you so hot and bothered?"

Caleb stared into the distance. "We've been friends for how many years, Abe? Since grade school if I remember rightly. We've always had each other's back." He turned to look at him. "Is there something you haven't told me?"

Abe looked away. "Not really. You know what's gone with me. Why?"

"Tracker handed me this as well. In it you'll find some interesting reading. They have discovered a pretty serious legitimate threat against you."

"What?" Abe turned disbelieving eyes on Caleb. "Now, wait a minute. We know that I can get threats all the time and they never pan out. They're always empty words."

Caleb was shaking his head. "Not this time, my friend. Tracker and her people are good. She's adamant that if there's a valid threat, you need to take precautions. From what her people have dug up, it's been out there for years, but it's now escalating."

Abe took the folder with a shaking hand. "That changes everything then, doesn't it? I can't stop doing what I do, you know that as well as I know. It's who I am. We'll just have to take more and more precautions and really screen who we deal with."

"I wish I felt it was that easy, Abe. Somehow I don't think it is. That episode with the sniper at the press conference? It wasn't Elizabeth he was after, it was Nathaniel. And then there's Matt. He is out to get to you through your men. I would warn Gideon and Rebecca as well. He'll try through them too."

Abe caught his breath. "That's a good point. I would never have connected Rebecca with the threats but he's shown he doesn't really care." He stopped speaking. "Now, about Elizabeth? What are we going to do about her?"

"Other than locking her into a room with no windows and us having the only key, I don't think we can keep her contained. She won't stand for it."

Abe nodded glumly. "I know. Neither her Dad nor Jake have been able to sway her. I have a feeling she's really going to go on the offensive and that scares me."

"Me, too. And we wouldn't be able to stop her. I know Nathaniel will be right there with her. Can you take him and leave him somewhere until this is over?"

Abe laughed. "Don't think so. He's gotten pretty attached to our sweet friend. They make a cute couple."

Caleb laughed as he turned to leave. "That they do."

Nathaniel stared at Elizabeth's back a few days later. "Not happening, Elizabeth. There is no way I'm leaving you to fight this guy on your own."

She refused to look at him. "You have to. Look what he's already done to you. I won't let it happen again."

"I'm not letting walk away, so let's get that straight." He placed his hands on her shoulders. "I won't beg you, Elizabeth. If you walk away, I will still be there, watching out for you. It's your choice if it's behind your back or by your side."

She shrugged away from him. "I've made my decision, Nathaniel. Please respect it. Don't come near me, now or in the future. I can't handle you or anyone else getting hurt on my behalf."

Nathaniel stopped her with a hand on her arm and turned her to face him. She refused to look at him. He stared at the ceiling, then down at her. "Elizabeth, I can't do that. I can't honour your wish that I stay away. It would tear me apart to let you walk away and then see you get hurt. Look at me." She refused to look up. He bent down enough he could see her face. "Look at me, please."

She raised her eyes to his, and shaking her head, said, "No, Nathaniel. Don't ask that of me."

He wrapped her in his arms. "Elizabeth, you're too much a part of me now to let you walk away. I won't. Too bad if you don't like it." He leaned back so he could watch her face. "I'm not going anywhere, Elizabeth, so get used to it."

She broke from him and ran. He followed her but she was too quick and was gone before he could get to her.

He stood, watching the dust from her car. Jake stoped beside him and contemplated the dust trail.

"Go after, boy. Don't let her run."

Nathaniel shook his head. "No, I can't. It would destroy what we have if I did. I'll find her later." He turned to walk away but Jake's hand on his arm stopped him.

"I have learned one thing in life, Nathaniel. Don't let the good ladies disappear from your life. Trust me. Go after her. I know her well. She'll run, but she's ready to fight. She needs you."

Nathaniel once again shook his head. "No, I can't, Jake. I know what she's not saying. She's been pushed too far by too many people right now and she needs her space."

Jake just shook his head and walked away. Nathaniel watched him, then turned once more to the road. He dug for his keys and headed for his vehicle. He would give it one more try. Lord, please let her hear me and understand what I am trying to say to her.

He stopped in her driveway. Her car was there. He hesitated, not knowing what to expect. She didn't answer her doorbell but he knew she was there. Heading around to the back yard, he found her, sitting knees up and clasped in her arms, head buried on them. He sank to the bench beside her and said nothing.

"Why are you here, Nathaniel? I told you to leave me alone."

"That I can't do, Elizabeth." He couldn't say what he really wanted, she wasn't ready. "Can we stop this dance and just decide to work together to find this guy?"

She turned her head to look at him, tears streaking her cheeks. "So, what makes you think we can find him when no one else can?"

"We have you. You want to put yourself out there as a target. Let's make a plan and see what we can do. You can't just go out there blindly without knowing what you want to do or accomplish. We can talk to Abe and the guys and see what they suggest." He searched her face. "Are you really ready to let Caleb not know what you're up to?"

"I am. I am so afraid that someone close to one of them is letting him know where I am and what I'm doing."

Nathaniel straightened. "That's something I don't think we ever did." He pulled her to her feet. "Come on. We're going on a search."

"A search? For what?"

"Bugs, trackers, tracers, GPS units, what have you. I don't remember hearing that we ever looked for them."

Two hours later, he set the last of the devices in the bag she held. "I don't know how he managed to place so many. It must have been while you were having the renovations done. He even got your car."

She nodded. "I'm afraid for my computer now. Can he have gotten at it?"

"It's possible. If you want, I can have Micah take a look at it for you."

"Yes, please. We might as well know the extent of everything. Do you want to give those to Caleb or to Eddie or to Frankie? None of them will be too happy."

Nathaniel contemplated the bag she held. "No, I don't suppose they will. I'll drop them off on my way home. Now, as to your plans, what are you thinking?"

"My plan? That was a bluff. I really have no plan.

I just wanted you to stay away.”

“Didn’t work, now did it, Ma’am?”

“Ma’am? We’re back to that?” At his nod, she smiled. “I still have to come up with a plan to counteract that. Life’s been too busy.”

Chapter 24

"You found these where?" Frankie stared into the bag at all the devices.

"Most of them in her home. A couple on her car."

Frankie shook his head. "I thought we had searched the house. That certainly slipped through the cracks."

Nathaniel's voice had a hard edge of anger. "And it could have killed her. I've gone everything, every room, every heat vent, every crack that I could find. All of these were there."

"It's no wonder he knew exactly where she was when she went out. Now to figure out how to trap him."

Nathaniel spoke as he turned on his heel. "Don't worry. We've come up with a plan. If it works you'll know. If it doesn't you'll know too."

Frankie stared at his back. "Now, wait a minute. What plan?"

Nathaniel shook his head as he walked away. "We're not telling anyone. That's the only way it can work."

Frankie watched him walk away, took a look at the bag in his hand and went to find Caleb. Caleb would be very unhappy to put it mildly, Frankie knew.

"All set?" Nathaniel took her duffle bag from her and locked the door after her.

"I am, Nathaniel." Elizabeth's eyes searched the neighbourhood. She could feel the evil near her. "Is Abe on board?"

"He is. So's the rest of the team. You've really won them over, you know that."

She looked surprised. "I thought the jury was still out on that one. It's come back in my favour, has it?"

"Big time. They just weren't sure on how to take you at first. You do come across differently than the women they're used to."

She started to laugh at that. "Yeah, right, considering Rebecca and don't forget Sarah, the electrician."

Nathaniel laughed with her as he shut the truck door behind her. He stood, also feeling the evil around them. "Now that we're on own way, and we've say our prayer, any second thoughts?"

She shook her head. "No, I think we're right in what we're doing. I just wish Caleb had been more approachable about it."

"Caleb is Caleb. He's responsible to the town and doesn't have the freedom that we do. He has to follow the rules and regulations. As long as we stay within the law, we're okay. He'll get over it."

"I hope so. We've been friends for so many years. I'm also friends with his wife, Hannah. I haven't got to see her much since I've been back." She turned to look at him. "Do we have a tail?"

"We do. Can you check this plate number with the list Jace gave us?"

"It's not on there. I'll see what Micah can dig up."

"It'll be him. I wonder what he'll do when we

leave the truck at the airport and disappear on a plane?"

She laughed. "Catch a plane maybe, but I doubt it. He won't know where we're going in time to stop us. Are you sure your friend's okay with flying us?"

"She is. She's done this for Abe before when we've had someone we've needed to get away real quick and Abe didn't want Ian to be the one doing the flying." He turned into the airport, tail still in place, and headed for the private hangars. Signing in, he drove towards a hangar near the end of the row.

"He couldn't get through. Let's hope we can be in the air before he figures out how to get the tail numbers."

Thirty minutes later, they were in the air and on their way. Nathaniel hadn't told Elizabeth where they were headed. He hadn't meant to keep her in the dark, it had just worked out that fast.

"So, where are we headed?" She turned her seat to look at him.

"Did I forget to tell you?" An innocent look came over his face, but the twinkle of fun in his eyes gave him away.

"No, you didn't, and you know I don't do surprises either."

He reached for her hand. "We're heading to where your parents are waiting. I talked to them and they flew out to the island last night."

"Island? Really?" She smiled with pleasure. "That's so sweet, Nathaniel. But are you ready for the third degree as to your intentions?"

He laughed. "I kind of gathered that would

happen. Elizabeth, you have come to mean so much to me. We've been pushed together, not by choice but by circumstances. I understand if you need time, but I have considered you my girl for weeks now. And so have the guys, you know. Will you go one step further and consider being my girl for life, bringing the music and the fun I've been lacking?"

She nodded through her tears. "You told me once that my kisses were mine to give. I give them to you, Nathaniel, my love."

He laughed as he shook his head. "You tell me that when I can't kiss you like I want to."

She smirked. "I've also come up with the way to counteract when you call me Ma'am."

"You have, have you? And what would that be?"

"A kiss each and every time." She sat back in her seat, a pleased look on her face.

Aaron watched the two of them closely as they ate. "How does the investigation stand?"

"Right now, it's going nowhere. We found numerous listening devices and trackers in Elizabeth's home and car. Frankie has them. He wasn't pleased to have them. That's one thing they never did do, search her home or car. I thought it had been done or I would have done it sooner."

"At least you've found them now." Miriam, her mother, spoke up. "Now, when do you head out for your next trip, Nathaniel?"

He shrugged. "It should have been this week but Abe called it off. There's something going on there too. He said Naomi from Tracker's had found some pretty credible threats."

"Yes, Naomi's one of the best. Not as good as Tracker but almost." He looked up with a grin at his daughter. "So, Whizz, how be we ask Abe and the other guys down here and bring in Nathaniel's family? A beach wedding would be nice." He laughed at her outraged cry.

"Dad, be nice. I just got engaged. I would like to enjoy it a bit, particularly as we have no ring yet." She glared at him. "And by the way, I hear I have you to thank for that nickname."

Her father started to laugh even harder. "You never knew?" She shook her head. "You are just so like that little sports car, you know."

"No, I'm not. You have everyone in town calling me that."

"I'm sorry, honey. I really didn't mean for that to happen."

"Yeah, right. And I love you too. May we be excused, Mom?" At her nod, she stood and reached for Nathaniel's hand. "Let's go. The "old folks" will get the dishes."

Nathaniel stood beside her as she sat on her favourite rock on the shoreline. "You're right. We haven't picked a ring yet. But I have this that my Grandmother gave me years ago and told me to hold on to for the right girl." He pulled a plain star sapphire ring from his shirt pocket. "I would be honoured if you would consider wearing it. It has a lot of history. But if you don't we'll find another one."

At her hesitation, he reached to put it back, but her hand stopped him. "No, Nathaniel, I would be the one honoured."

Later, she asked, "Did you hear what Dad said about your team and your family?"

"I did. It's just not the right timing for us, as much as I would love to do just that. We'll keep it in mind though for possibilities." He noticed her shiver. "Let's go in."

"No, I'm not cold. He's found us, you know. I can feel the evil."

Nathaniel hugged her close. "I can too. Let's go in."

Chapter 25

A be kept his head down to his work, but he could hear Nathaniel pacing his office. "Sit, Nathaniel. What's up?"

"Somehow, he found us when we were on the island. How do we stop this guy?"

"He found you, even with the precautions we took?" Abe sat back, staring at the pen he was twisting in his hand. "How? We were so careful."

"He followed us to the airport. He shouldn't have been able to read the tail numbers or find out where we were going. So how did he? And how do we stop him?"

"I can't explain that. We were so careful." He leaned forward. "Micah, come here. Did you find anything of Elizabeth's computer?"

"Nothing that would track anything, if that's what you're asking, but I did find a program buried that would track her emails and website visits. If she was on that before you left and said anything, that's how he found you."

Nathaniel leaned his head back and closed his eyes. "She was emailing her Mom about the plans. She would never have thought not to."

"This guy is good, but we're better. Now, how do we stop him?"

"We go public with our engagement. That would draw him out."

Abe shook his head. "Absolutely not. We're not using either one of you that way. Although word will get out soon enough unless you hide her finger every time she's around someone." Abe's sense of humour just had to come through once in a while.

"Funny, Abe, we would if we could. No, we need to come up with a plan, and if we don't she will."

"That's what I'm afraid of, Nathaniel. Whizz of old had some pretty wicked plans."

"I heard it was you, Abe and Doug that did."

Abe smiled. "She was the instigator in a lot of them but because she was a girl, we took the fall for her."

"Don't let her hear you say that. The only thing I can come up with is that we're seen out together more than we have been. She hasn't said if she's had any more notes or packages."

"I don't think she has." Abe looked at his phone as it dinged. "That's Caleb. He just got a note that went to Elizabeth. She's fighting mad on this one. Come on, Nathaniel. Let's get you where you can calm your girl down."

Elizabeth stood in front of her living room window, tense, angry. Nathaniel stood beside her, contemplating the night and waiting for her to speak.

"I'm going to do it, Nathaniel. I'm going to meet with this guy, but on my terms and where I choose. He's not winning at that." She looked up at him.

"I know you are. So does everyone else. I'm not letting you go alone, though. I'm in this with you."

She nodded. "I know you are. Now, let's set up some plans and see if we can flush him out." She turned to face Abe and Caleb. Eddie she knew as on his way. Frankie was going back over timelines with the crime lab techs.

"What have you come up with, Caleb?" She went right to the point, her eyes narrowed as she stared at him.

"I don't like that you want to meet with him, Elizabeth."

"You really don't have a choice in this, Caleb. Give me much of a hassle and I'll walk from this room and go meet him tonight."

"Don't make threats like that. They won't work, and you know better." Caleb was quickly losing his temper, and that he never did. He turned away before he said anything else.

"Abe?" Elizabeth turned to him next.

"I think you have the right idea." At Caleb's protest, Abe held up his hand. "Just wait a minute, Caleb. She's brought you in as a courtesy. She doesn't have to do that at all. She could meet with him and settle it without law enforcement involvement, and you know it."

Eddie spoke up. "Yes, she can, but she wants our input. We need to put aside that fact that we're friends and look at this as it is, someone who wants to hurt Elizabeth. That, that's what we need to be dealing with, not whether or not she can do it on her own." Eddie kept his eyes on Caleb. "What are your ideas, Abe?"

"Elizabeth has come up with a place to meet. I agree that it will work. I can have my guys surrounding the clearing, and they won't be seen. I would suggest that we stake it out well ahead of time.

Elizabeth has a number to contact him with, and she'll do that shortly before she wants to meet with him. If he doesn't agree to meet with her at the place and time she states, she walks away and lets you take over."

Caleb had turned as Abe was speaking. "Will this work?"

Abe shrugged. "Who knows? We're running out of options, is all I can say."

"Where do you want to meet him, Elizabeth?" Caleb waited for her to speak, knowing he had been out of line, and not speaking as the police chief he was.

She handed him a map. "Here. It has the best cover for Abe's men, enough openness that I should be safe. There's really only one way in."

He nodded. "That's all true, but if it's who you think it is, he had some good hunting and tracking skills."

"No, not really. He had you guys all fooled. He would never have been able to survive on his own in the wild. He could barely survive in an urban environment. I doubt he's changed that much. He's too lazy to do much."

"You really don't like him, do you?" Caleb raised an eyebrow at her. "What's the story? I thought you at least tolerated him."

"Catch him and I might tell you. Let's say, I never trusted him. He reminds me of a slimy little snake that everyone wants to get rid of."

"Elizabeth, that's not nice." Nathaniel's voice came from behind her.

"Trust me, Nathaniel, that's exactly what he's like. Ask any of the girls we hung around with. They all have the same opinion." She turned to him. "You'll see."

He nodded. "I take your word for it. Now, when and how?"

Abe spoke up. "We know the where. We'll need to work out the logistics of it and that will take a few days. Unfortunately, we can't do it before Friday or Saturday. We're out of town for a couple of days. And don't try it on your own, Whizz."

"I promise I won't. Just get back as quickly as you can."

Chapter 26

"Everyone ready and in place?" Abe's voice was soft over their radios. An affirmative came from the five men around the clearing Elizabeth had chosen. Micah sat in the command centre intent on his computer screens. Elizabeth and Nathaniel stood in the centre of the clearing, Elizabeth nervous, glancing occasionally around. Abe knew Caleb had men stationed near by. They had spent time in prayer over this and felt confident in moving ahead.

"What time did you tell him, Elizabeth?" Nathaniel's voice was low.

"I told him to be here for 2 p.m. and if he wasn't here by 2:15, I was done. He never liked threats, always wanting to be the one giving the threats."

"And you're positive it's him?"

"I am. He's the only one I know who could be this vicious."

A snapping of a branch turned their attention to the far side of the clearing. A shadowy form hovered there.

"Come out and show yourself, Robert Larson. I know it's you. Stop hiding."

The form didn't move and Elizabeth repeated herself.

The form moved forward, stepping slowing and carefully. An arm was bent at an angle and almost useless.

"So, you're going to show yourself, are you? Why?" Elizabeth's voice was harsh.

"Why, you ask? How dare you ask that? You've taken everything I worked for."

"No, you did that to yourself. You have no one to blame. So why pick on me and the other four?"

Robert was shaking with rage as he stumbled closer. "You took everything. You had to be first, to be the best."

Elizabeth shook her head. "No, Robert, that's not how it was. You had the ability, the skill, but you chose to use it wrong. You chose to do the drugs, the alcohol. No one forced you to that." She paused, then continued, "So why the threats, the letters?"

"You needed to be taught a lesson. You needed to learn what it's like to live in fear, just like I do." He stared harder at her, eyes not wavering even when Nathaniel made a move.

Nathaniel sensed something else was going on and scanned the area around them. He couldn't speak to let Abe know what he was feeling. He just prayed that he was wrong.

"Who else are you working for, Robert? You're not smart enough to have come up with this all on your own. At least not the last few months' worth. So who's the other man?"

He shook his head. "See, that's what I mean. You downplay what I'm capable of."

She studied him with sadness. "No, Robert, you're not smart enough to do all this planning. You never were. You tried to fit in, but never could. You chased people away from you." She raised her hand in the signal she had worked out with Abe. "It's over,

Robert. It ends tonight."

"No, it doesn't." A weapon appeared in his hand. "Tonight, it's over for you."

"No, it's not Robert. It doesn't have to end this way. Who put you up to this?" Elizabeth was not backing away from trying to get to the core of who was really after her. She knew it wasn't Robert.

A sudden movement from Robert had Nathaniel taking her to the ground and covering her, weapon in hand. He could hear the chatter over his radio as he searched the area.

Robert lay still, blood covering his back. Nathaniel gathered Elizabeth up and hurried her from the area to the safety of their command centre.

Caleb's eyes searched. "Who?"

Abe shook his head. "It wasn't one of my men, that's for sure. We would have taken him alive. I think Elizabeth was getting to him. Now, we may never know who it really was."

"I think we will. I have a team at the house where he's been living. We finally got that address tonight. It was so well hidden, it's taken all this time."

They both turned as Frankie approached them. "Nothing?"

He shook his head. "Whoever it was knows the woods. He didn't leave a track at all."

Cale shook his head. "I just wish for once to have a straightforward investigation." He paused as his phone rang. "Excuse, guys, let me get this." He walked away and looked down. Hannah. "Hi, favourite girl, what's wrong?"

"Oh Caleb, He's done it again."

Caleb stopped walked and squeezed his eyes closed. God had given another name to his wife. *I had so hoped it wouldn't happen again, Lord, but You know best.* "Who is it?"

Her voice was barely above a whisper as she spoke the name. Caleb turned to stare around the area, feeling eyes on him. Did this man know he was next to be taken down?

Frankie and Abe watched as Caleb tucked his phone back into his pocket.

"That doesn't look good." Abe spoke both their thoughts.

"No. I would hazard a guess Hannah's come up with a name."

"A name?" Abe couldn't believe he was hearing this.

Frankie nodded. "She's come up with names in the past, who are the ones we've arrested. God gives them to her. He didn't with Matt and Sarah, but it looks like He did today." He paused as Caleb stopped walking beside them. "Who'd she give you?"

"How'd you know?"

"You have the same look as before. Hannah came through?"

Caleb nodded and gave the name. The men looked at one another, then sighed.

"Let's go find the evidence we need." Frankie turned to walk away.

"Keep those two close to your guys for the next couple of days, at least until we can arrest this man."

Abe nodded. "They won't be going anywhere."

Chapter 27

Elizabeth sat at her piano, working on lyrics she had promised to have done two weeks ago. *Your mercy, Lord,* she thought. *We don't deserve it, but You give it.* She turned those thoughts into words and then sat back. *Yes, Peter would be happy* she thought. With his tune and her lyrics, she prayed God would reach many.

She turned as Caleb and Abe entered, Nathaniel on their heels, faces grim.

"Now what, Caleb? I'm not leaving my home again."

Caleb shook his head. "You don't have to. We have the man behind it."

She looked startled, then nodded. "Gus Young."

Caleb nodded. "I don't know how you figured it out, but you're right."

She shrugged. "It had to be him. He was always getting Robert to do his dirty work for him. Gus had such talent, he's really much better than I am, and Mrs. C. knew that. He just didn't want to work his way up to the top, he wanted to start at the top. It doesn't work that way, unfortunately, so he blamed anyone who got ahead faster than he did."

"If you knew the name, why didn't you say something?"

She looked up at him, then at Abe, finally centering her gaze on Nathaniel. "I wasn't sure, not until you walked in right now. I knew there was someone back there in the shadows." She looked down at the keyboard. "You've arrested him?"

"We have, Elizabeth. We have a lot of documents to go through and the investigation into him is just starting." Caleb turned to leave. "We still haven't found out who killed Robert. Gus denies it."

"No, he didn't do it." The men stared at her.

"Do you know who did, Whizz?" Abe's voice was gentle as he spoke to his old friend.

"Nothing definite, just a vague impression."

"And we know now that the sniper wasn't Robert, so we still have that out there." Abe was truly puzzled at that. "I just don't know who that would be."

After Abe and Caleb had left, Nathaniel sat on the piano bench beside her and idly picked out notes. "Care to share who you think it was?"

She started to shake her head, then stopped. "I'm not sure if I should tell you. Mercy says I don't, that I let it go. Truth tells me I need to say the name." She looked at him, tears in her eyes. "If I tell you, will you tell Abe and Caleb?"

"If it's just speculation at the moment, no. There was no evidence anyone else was there."

She looked down, sorrow in her face. "In six months or so, I promise I will tell Caleb and Abe. I think it was Jake. He always wanted to protect me, wrap me in bubble wrap so no harm came to me. He looked at me as the daughter they could never have." She sighed. "Jake told me he only has about three or four months left to live. He has never said anything about Robert, but I'm sure that's who it was. We would never be able to prove it."

"He's that good he could get in and out and not leave a trace? That good with a rifle?"

She nodded. "He is. He's been hunting those woods for so many years, he could."

She leaned into his hug, her tears soaking into his shirt. "Why, Nathaniel? Why did this have to happen?"

He rested his chin on her soft blond hair. "I don't think we'll ever really know here on earth, sweet thing, but I do know that what you've been through has come through in the lyrics you write. There's a depth to them that isn't in a lot of music today. What you have lived has translated to words. God still has a powerful voice to work through you."

She thought about his words. "God's mercy has been strong on my mind. We don't deserve His love, His compassion, His way to eternal life, but He gives it so freely. His forgiveness is such that we will never fully understand it until we stand in heaven." She leaned back. "Now that we have the deep theological discussions out of the way, and I've finished my work that I needed to do, what shall we do for the day?"

He grinned, then spoke, "Let's go see Greg and plan a wedding."

She laughed. "I like the way you think, Nathaniel."

Epilogue

Three months later, she sat once again on her favourite rock on the island, wind idly blowing her hair. Nathaniel stood and watched, then moved towards her, encircling her with his arms.

They remained like that for a while, watching the sun as it sank, streaking the sky with its red and purple and pink ribbons.

Elizabeth spoke. "I can never get enough sunsets or sunrises. There is just something about the start of the day or the end of the day that impresses me with how God loves us."

"I agree, sweet thing. God has given us so much." He looked down at her face. "Have you thought any more about talking with Caleb?"

She nodded. "I need to. Now that Jake has gone, I need to finish up that bit of the investigation. He left me a letter to give to Caleb. I'm sure it will explain it all." She sighed. "I just hope Caleb understands."

"I'm sure he will. Come on, let me take you out to dinner. Your parents will be down later tonight and my family coming in tomorrow. This is the last chance we'll have for a few days of quiet."

She laughed as she slipped down from the rock. "Be nice, Nathaniel. Your team's leaving us alone for a few days. When do you go out again?"

"Next week." He looked down at her. "Did we ever set a wedding date?"

She laughed. "You know we did. There's still work to do to get to that point."

He stopped her. "Wedding day or not coming up, I am glad you are in my life. Keep me grounded, Elizabeth. Keep being the friend, Whizz, to those around you. Keep God foremost in your life and your lyrics."

She looked up at him. "I would say the same to you but you don't write lyrics." He laughed at her nonsense. "I would say to keep those you guard safe. I pray you never ever have to be the sniper you've trained to be. God is merciful, my love. He can grant our prayers."

Dear Readers

Mercy? What really is it? To each person, it is something different. I will let you each decide what it means to you.

God's mercy to us shows through in so many ways. His forgiveness is there for the asking, and how often we fail to ask. Let that thought remain with you, that all you have to do is bow before Him and ask. He's already granted it.

Nathaniel and Elizabeth - quite the pair. Their story was a difficult one to write in incorporating mercy towards those who had them in their sights. My Dad played the piano, honky-tonk he always called it. One of the hymns I so enjoyed hearing him play was Love Divine. Mom always said it sounded like bells when he would play the treble portion. That's the song that I referred to as the song with the bells. Another favourite hymns is Master, The Tempest is Raging, which is the thunder song Drew asked for. I loved to hear the voices of the men singing so strong, yet dropping to a whisper. I could picture the boat on the sea, the fear of the disciples, the calming of the storm with just one outreached hand. God's mercy is that to me—He can calm the raging storm around and within me. My part is to accept His forgiveness. In accepting His forgiveness, I also need to forgive others. That is what I have tried so hard to portray with Nathaniel and Elizabeth.

The story will continue with another of Abe's team. Tracker, the lovely lady who turned up in this book, isn't done. She'll be back. Stay tuned as to whose lady she really is.

God bless each one of you as you read. Continue to study His word and be the light in the world we are called to be.

Ronna